UNICORN SEEKERS

UNICORN SEEKERS

THE NIGHT OF THE UNICORN DANCE

CERRIE BURNELL

ILLUSTRATED BY KAYT BOCHENSKI

■SCHOLASTIC

Published in the UK by Scholastic, 2024
1 London Bridge, London, SE1 9BG
Scholastic Ireland, 89E Lagan Road, Dublin Industrial Estate,
Glasnevin, Dublin, D11 HP5F

SCHOLASTIC and associated logos are trademarks and/or
registered trademarks of Scholastic Inc.

Text © Cerrie Burnell, 2024
Cover illustration © Lucy Fleming, 2024
Interior illustrations © Kayt Bochenski, 2024

The right of Cerrie Burnell to be identified
as the author of this work has been asserted by her
under the Copyright, Designs and Patents Act 1988.

ISBN 978 0702 32395 9

A CIP catalogue record for this book
is available from the British Library.

Printed in Great Britain by Clays Ltd, Elcograf S.p.A.
Paper made from wood grown in sustainable forests
and other controlled sources.

MIX
Paper | Supporting
responsible forestry
FSC
www.fsc.org   FSC® C018072

1 3 5 7 9 10 8 6 4 2

This is a work of fiction. Names, characters, places, incidents
and dialogues are products of the author's imagination or are used
fictitiously. Any resemblance to actual people, living or dead,
events or locales is entirely coincidental.

www.scholastic.co.uk

In shining memory of Skylar,
who knew every horse was secretly a unicorn.

Dear Unicorn Seeker

Thank you for stopping by our awesome blog!

We are four lovely friends who are actual, authentic Unicorn Seekers. We've all seen unicorns on our doorsteps, in our gardens and even in bathtubs.

First, let us tell you the story of how we discovered a UNICORN in a South London park last autumn. This wasn't just any unicorn – she was pretty extraordinary, luminous as the moon and quite alarming, and she was just a baby. Think super cute but totally unpredictable. Like a cross between a mountain goat and a wildcat.

Her name was Stormy, and she was the colour of snowstorms and wishes. Her horn was as beautiful as enchanted ice, and if she accidentally caught you with it – it hurt! Like, a lot.

She belonged to a glory called Winter's Dawn, who live in snowy, glacial climates and spend a long time in freezing water, almost like a mer-horse. She was the most magical little soul we'd ever met.

But Stormy's fierce and graceful mum, Lumi, was in serious trouble! She'd been kidnapped by these two Scandinavian guys, who were also excellent musicians. And Stormy's bold and beautiful dad, Dash, was being lured into danger by the same musical guys, which was totally not cool.

Their kidnappings were part of a dark plan to capture Stormy, because a baby unicorn's horn holds the most powerful magic. But with the help of our fabulous friend Rishi, and his chai-latte-loving mum, along with Elodie's mum, Esme (the original Unicorn Seeker!), we managed to save the day, set the family of unicorns free AND help cure a beloved guide dog along the way.

It was hard to say goodbye to Stormy though – to watch her dip and dive beneath the waves. All our hearts cracked a little bit as she swam away. But we feel better knowing that she's safe with Lumi and Dash, living her best underwater life in the cold Iceland Sea.

We still miss her so much, but now we're focused on rescuing more unicorns – and we'd love YOUR help.

We know there are Unicorn Seekers all over the world who are just waiting to discover their gifts. Maybe you dream of unicorns? Perhaps you've spotted a unicorn's shadow when everyone else saw a horse? Or maybe you've even seen a real-life unicorn behind the recycling bins?

Just remember – anyone can see a unicorn if the weather is right! And if you want to make friends with one, always carry gluten-free muffins, dandelions or thistles, as these are their fave foods. They adore moonlight and respond to LOVE, so always be welcoming and respectful.

Keep seeking with an open heart, and if you ever find a unicorn that needs help, please get in touch through the comments section of this blog.

Yours faithfully,

Elodie, Caleb, Marnie-Mae, Kit and Rishi

AKA The Unicorn Seekers of South London

CHAPTER ONE

SUNSHINE AND SAUSAGE ROLLS

In the vast city of London, where the sky can turn from brightest blue to golden grey in the blink of a dreamer's eye, just south of the great misty river and close to a lovely leafy park, Elodie Lightfoot was beginning to awake.

A soft summer dawn seeped beneath her curtains and Elodie blinked her sleepy brown eyes. As she turned over, a tiny zap of lightning quietly fizzed in her hair and she grinned. Elodie loved that she had her own little lightning storm in the ends of her dancing curls. Her hair was a heap of spiralling ringlets, which were mostly brown but occasionally glittered blue, especially if a unicorn was near.

The cosy second-floor flat where she lived with

her dad and her maman was peaceful and still. The only sound was her dad, Max, whistling softly in the kitchen, where he was mixing, baking and icing gluten-free cakes and treats for the day ahead. Max always rose at six minutes after sunrise so he'd be ready to leave on time to set up the Feather and Fern coffee van.

Elodie stretched and smiled as the flickering memory of her dream came back to her. It had been of Stormy and her proud and beautiful parents, all arching majestically through the wild waves of the Iceland Sea. Little Stormy's horn had shone with the luminous glitter of sea-light, and in its strange and eerie glow Elodie thought she'd caught a glimpse of a mermaid.

"I hope you're all happy," she murmured to herself, trying to ignore the tug of sadness that pulled at her heart whenever she thought of saying goodbye to them last autumn.

But Elodie knew, deep down, that the family of Winter's Dawn unicorns were safe and free, and that was all that truly mattered, even if she missed them terribly.

She sat up in bed and flung the curtains wide open, letting the morning light flood in. Spring had blended into summer, with the tall, swaying trees around the lake budding beautifully with creamy hawthorn blossoms and a richness of green leaves. The day was cloudy but warm.

Elodie peered at her moon dial clock and saw she had woken early. In the long years when her beloved maman had lived in Paris, performing top-secret Unicorn Seeker duties, Elodie always left the flat one hour and six minutes after sunrise with her dad.

Since Maman had come home, Elodie didn't really need to leave so early. She could stay and listen to Maman's soothing singing as they sipped mint tea together and ate any misshapen chocolate croissants.

Yet sometimes Elodie still loved to hop, step and skip into the new day with her dad, helping him get ready to sell delicious treats to all of South London.

Today was one of those days.

She got dressed and twisted her mass of glorious curls into a thick plait, taking care not to catch her fingers on the little crackles of lightning that glimmered and sparked. But when Elodie peered at herself in the mirror the plait was all a bit messy. She sighed and reached into her overcrowded bookcase, where a little pot of lotion that had belonged to her great-grandmother, Elyse de Lyon, was carefully wedged behind a collection of Celtic fairy tales.

The pot was the colour of rust and silver, and looked like it was centuries old. It had a mythical winged horse embossed upon its lid.

Not mythical, Elodie thought with a smile. *Real.*

Slowly she unscrewed the lid. At once the entire room filled with the aroma of rain on a midsummer's eve, then she breathed in the rushing saltiness of the sea, followed by the swift smell of frost. Lastly came Elodie's favourite scent of all: moonlight.

She took the tiniest pinch of lotion, which was as cold as snow to touch, shook out her messy plait and smoothed the lotion through her hair, marvelling at her reflection as her beautiful curls obeyed and glided into a neat plait.

After carefully closing the lid and returning the lotion to its place on the bookcase, Elodie picked up her backpack, looped her rainbow-laced roller skates over her shoulder and walked happily into the cinnamon-scented kitchen to steal a lavender cupcake for breakfast.

"Great timing, Elle!" her dad, Max, beamed at her. "I've made extra vegan sausage rolls this morning. I could definitely use some help getting them to the van."

Elodie nodded, shoving the lavender cupcake into her mouth and grabbing as much as she could carry.

Out of the door and down the creaky steps they tiptoed with bags of almond croissants and gluten-free gingerbread hearts, jars of jasmine syrup, boxes of blueberry and lavender delights, baskets of sparkly buns and vegan sausage rolls, and plenty of organic oat milk.

Elodie took special care to step over Pirate, the large bad-tempered cat who belonged to Mrs Singh, their kind and lovely downstairs neighbour. Pirate was dozing on the bottom step. He glared at them with his one eye, but luckily didn't scratch anyone.

Elodie paused for a moment, staring back up the stairs. She was almost willing Mrs Singh, who was eighty-seven and another highly gifted seeker, to emerge sleepily from her flat to tell Elodie about a unicorn she'd met in her dreams. But the hallway remained still and quiet, apart from Pirate's disgruntled snores.

Elodie followed Max out into the clear, bright morning. The air felt as crisp as new apples and, though the sun shone warmly, a cool breeze came twirling down the street, tugging playfully at Elodie's plait.

"Perfect weather for croissants," Max said with a wink, and Elodie rolled her eyes.

"You say that every morning, Dad," she groaned as they crossed the empty street and slipped through the rusted gate of the leafy park.

Elodie adored this time of morning when everything felt possible. The boating lake was a beautiful shade of blue and full of sleek-necked swans, the grass was dotted with the brightness of daisies and, in the clear summer sunlight, if she stared hard enough, Elodie could almost imagine that the ancient statues scattered throughout the park were real.

If only they were, she thought longingly, remembering the way she'd once mistaken a beautiful midnight unicorn, Astra, for a statue of a little black horse.

A bright-winged parakeet swooped overhead, squeaking joyfully, and Elodie set to work helping Max open up the Feather and Fern. The van itself was dazzling green and cluttered with recycled coffee cups, biodegradable napkins and a huge bubbling espresso machine. But Elodie knew that there was room to hide a unicorn in the back if they ever really needed to.

Suddenly the sound of whooshing wheels reached her ears, and Elodie leapt out of the van, kicked off her shoes and pulled on her faded dusky-mauve skates.

"Marnie-Mae!" she screamed, all but flying into her best friend's arms.

Marnie-Mae's braided hair was a fabulous shade

of violet, and her beloved skates were leopard print. She was an excellent skater and a fearless protector of unicorns, just like Elodie.

"Girls, not so fast!" called Marnie's mum, Joni, as the two friends collided into a cuddle and fell laughing to the ground.

"Morning, Joni," said Max, handing her a decaf mocha, and Joni grinned appreciatively.

"Have a wonderful day, my love."

She beamed, planting a kiss on Marnie's forehead. Then Joni turned and strode away up the little hill to the train station in her rather magnificent gold high heels, making her way to the city, where she worked in publicity for a make-up company.

"Let's skate round the maze!" cried Marnie. "I bet it's empty at this time of the morning."

Elodie nodded and glided away after her friend. As she moved gracefully along the track that led to the maze, she was warmed by the sunshine. Then all of a sudden Elodie felt her heartbeat quicken, like the pounding rhythm of a horse's hooves. It was as if something powerful and bright was rushing towards her.

"Come on, Elle!" yelled Marnie-Mae, beckoning to her impatiently.

Something caught Elodie's eye, and she skidded to a stop. For a fleeting moment, Elodie thought she had glimpsed the shadow of a galloping horse. She put one of her stoppers down and spun slowly on the spot, blinking her hazel-brown eyes, taking in the butterflies and morning blackbirds.

There was no sign of any horse. The shadow had vanished. Perhaps it was just her wild imagination or her heart being hopeful. Either way, the park was the same as ever.

CHAPTER TWO
ECHOES AND SHADOWS

At the entrance to the maze, which had been formed from large leafy hedges and tall bushes, Elodie was greeted by the gentle howl of a sleepy St Bernard dog. He had curled himself in a huge furry ball beneath the shade of a blossoming wild cherry tree.

"Rufus!" She smiled, gliding round him in a perfect half-moon, before halting and crouching down to ruffle his warm, floppy ears.

"He didn't sleep well," said a familiar voice.

Elodie glanced up to see her friend Kit approaching on his roller blades, a pencil tucked behind his ear and his purposefully plain notebook stuffed in his hoody pocket, which Elodie knew was actually full of amazing unicorn facts.

Kit and his brother, Caleb, were Unicorn Seekers too. They were both homeschooled, something that Elodie and Marnie deeply envied. To spend your days visiting museums, soaking up art and history, studying and sketching the coots on the lake, or reading great literature in famous libraries ... it all sounded like a dream to both girls.

This also meant that Kit and Caleb were excellent at gathering new knowledge on unicorns. *And* they were amazing skaters. The two boys preferred roller blades, as they were apparently faster and cooler, and better for tricks, though Elodie and Marnie-Mae did not agree.

"Rufus was up all night with Caleb," Kit explained as Marnie-Mae came zooming over to join them.

"I bet Caleb is super excited about your half-term trip to Italy," she said. "I know I wouldn't be able to sleep if I was going to Milan!"

Kit shrugged. "Maybe. Caleb often has trouble sleeping anyway, but this time it seemed more to do with his dreams."

"What sort of dreams?" asked Elodie, standing up. "Like bad dreams or ones filled with unicorns?"

Kit shrugged. "Not really sure – he was too grumpy to go into it."

"So where is he? Maybe we could ask him," Marnie-Mae suggested, but Kit chuckled and shook his head.

"He's kind of busy right now," he said, pointing to a nearby bench where Caleb was sound asleep, hugging his roller blades to his chest.

Dreams were a big deal to the Unicorn Seekers, and Caleb, like Elodie and Mrs Singh, was particularly sensitive to unicorns. If ever a unicorn was in danger or trouble, or even just lost, they could make contact by visiting you in a dream. It was the way Dash had first found them.

Elodie was desperate to know more, to check if Caleb had sensed any hint of another unicorn. But she knew that disturbing him might not be the best plan...

"It can wait," she said. "Are you both coming to Oak Grove to hang out with Rishi after school today?"

Kit grinned. "We sure are."

"Great! We can talk about it then!" cried Marnie impatiently as she zipped off in a zigzag of speed and grace into the maze. "But right now, we race!"

In a flurry of yells and laughter, the three friends dipped and swerved along leafy paths lined with small pebbles and sprouting dandelions. The track spiralled into the centre of the maze where a little stone waterfall marked the middle.

Elodie yelped as Kit cut superbly across her, almost knocking Marnie-Mae over as he fought to get in front. But Marnie was still quicker. Years of ballet and karate had made her fearless and, even when she stumbled or fell, she shot straight back up and powered onwards.

Elodie let her wheels slow, carefully skimming over the tiny stones and admiring a clump of daisies while her two friends scrambled ahead. As Kit skated one way where the path forked, and Marnie-Mae glided down the other track, a pale-winged butterfly danced past Elodie and she smiled, charmed by its glittering wings.

All at once, her hair began to ever so softly crackle, and jagged bolts of wild blue light zapped through to the end of her plait. Elodie stopped still, her heart racing as she looked left then right, trying to see if there was anything nearby. Had the shadow she'd spotted earlier on followed her?

Elodie lingered, willing a unicorn to appear. But the maze was serene and soft in the morning sunlight. She blinked a few times, shaking away the magic in her hair.

And that was when she heard it – a little whinny, light-hearted and playful, echoing through the maze. Clear as the call of a parakeet.

Elodie spun round in amazement, her eyes wide open as the patter of hooves over pebbles reached her ears. Suddenly the air seemed full of sand – a rich pale sand, soft like silk, that floated to the ground like stardust.

There was no sign of a horse or unicorn though.

With a sigh, Elodie turned and raced to the middle of the maze. Kit and Marnie-Mae were already there, sitting cross-legged on the dusty ground beneath the fountain having an arm wrestle. It was obvious that both of them were certain they'd won the race, and this seemed like the best way to settle it. However, they both froze just as Elodie reached them.

Kit and Marnie-Mae blinked in hushed disbelief at the sound of whinnying.

"Where's it coming from?" Marnie-Mae whispered.

Kit put a finger to his lips, at once becoming very serious. As silently as he could, he rose to his feet and tiptoed on his blades to a little tunnel, vanishing wordlessly into it.

There came a startled little snort and then the fast-paced clatter of hooves.

Marnie and Elodie exchanged a hopeful look. But moments later a crestfallen Kit re-emerged, brushing clumps of dust and dandelion buds from his clothes.

"I definitely saw something," he told them. "Or rather *it* saw *me*. I saw the shadow of a little horse rearing up. Then it bolted, I chased after it, but I fell and when I got back up it had gone."

"Any sign of a horn? Like, any at all?" asked Marnie-Mae in a giddy voice.

Kit shook his head in disappointment. Elodie noticed that, as well as dust and dandelion buds, he had a dusting of fine golden sand on his clothes.

"The horns probably don't show up on shadows," she said thoughtfully, trying to remember. "I can ask my mum..." The other two nodded.

A little alarm went off on Marnie-Mae's waterproof watch, which she'd saved up for. After their adventure in Iceland with Stormy, she'd been determined to be more prepared the next time a unicorn vanished underwater. The watch also had a tiny in-built camera; she couldn't make videos or reels, but she could take pics at least.

"Time to get back to the Feather and Fern," Marnie-Mae said with a sigh.

With that, they all turned in unison and glided out of the maze to the dozing Rufus and sweetly dreaming Caleb. Kit flopped down on to the bench beside his brother, grinning at him.

"I guess it'll be a slow start for Caleb, but that's OK. We've got art first thing – we're sketching the swans."

The other two scowled at him, a little jealously, but Kit just shrugged in response.

"We still have to do maths and science," he said apologetically.

"Yeah, yeah," said Elodie, "but you get to be outside *all day*."

"Anyway, we'll see you at the Oak Grove garden later," said Kit.

He waved goodbye as the two girls flew across the park back to South London's best coffee van, where Esme Lightfoot, Elodie's maman, was waiting to walk them to school, an apricot croissant in her hand.

"We thought we saw a unicorn," Marnie-Mae blurted out, always eager to be getting on with the actual seeking.

Esme listened carefully as they told her about hearing the horse and seeing a shadow.

"It's very possible that a unicorn may appear to have the shadow of a horse," said Esme. "It's one of the best ways they stay hidden. Some glories are better at it than others. But the park is also full of deer at this time of year..."

Elodie was quiet as they walked to school. It was true: there were baby deer everywhere, but that didn't explain the lightning softly crackling in her curls ... nor the presence of sand.

THE PALACE OF CRYSTAL
INFORMATION FORUM

Your go-to place for events, community picnics, volunteer gardening, park maintenance, parakeet nesting and general news.

Perfect day out

My family and I recently discovered this beautiful, historical park and we will definitely be visiting again! Such a great day out. My daughter LOVED the dinosaur statues, and my wife and I adored the organic coffee from the cute little coffee van by the lake. So delicious.

@TwoTiredMums

Discoveries by the lake

My son was delighted to spot mallards, baby coots, cygnets and even cormorant at the lake last week. We also enjoyed the gluten-free treats from the

Feather and Fern. My son spotted some footprints in the mud by the lake shore. They looked like shells. Anyone know what they might be?

@BirdSpotterBill

Shell-shaped prints

Hey @BirdSpotterBill – my kids definitely came across something similar when they visited the park with their granddad. I was working on a big home renovation, but they took pics to show me. At first, we laughed, thinking they were made by a child's toy, maybe an electric horse?! But my kids found them all over the park, some especially close to the sports centre. Am really curious – I'd love to know where they came from!

@DreamDesignSuzy

Dinosaur dreaming

Hey, hey!

Has anyone considered it might an actual dinosaur! Ha ha! That would be so cool. Also, I love the Feather and Fern – that place is awesome.

But seriously though – I play a lot of beach volleyball and those weird prints are all over the sand. Hope to find out what weird creature's making them – keep me posted.

@AlwaysAtTheBeach

CHAPTER THREE
FOOTPRINTS IN THE SAND

By the time the school bell chimed for the end of the day, Elodie had had three sparkling – but very strange – daydreams.

The first one happened at break time. She was playing a game of tag and suddenly, just for a wild, windswept moment, she glimpsed a huge golden beach before her with a summer-bright sea. But then she blinked and found herself back in the grey concrete school playground.

The second time was during story time. The class were taking turns to read out loud a book about a girl who followed a white rabbit into a well. Elodie closed her eyes to listen to the magic of the story – except instead of white rabbits, she saw the white surf of breaking waves and heard the beating hooves of a horse.

A crackle of blue lightning zipped through her hair and she sat up to attention, wondering what that had meant, quietly hoping with all her heart that a unicorn might be near. Yet, as she gazed around a little forlornly, she could see no sign of one.

The third time, Elodie was fetching some extra pencils for art class, sent by her teacher to the storeroom by the head teacher's office. The corridor had been dark and peaceful, broken up by patches of sunlight slanting in through the high windows.

Elodie peered up to gaze at a tiny bird perched on the windowsill. As she did so, a shadow fell across her face. Her heart quickened. Her hair began to tingle and fizz. This time she knew exactly what it meant. A unicorn was trying to reach her! All the signs were there and she felt it deep in her bones.

Elodie turned, desperate to study the shadow on the wall opposite the windows. It was horse-shaped, wondrous and fast.

Definitely not a deer.

Its ears were poised like those of a cat, and for a fragment of a heartbeat Elodie was certain she'd glimpsed a dark shadowy horn between them.

Seeming to sense Elodie's attention, the shadow suddenly fled. She grabbed a chair and strained to see out of the window, but it was too high and all she was left with was the echo of hooves clattering across the playground.

It doesn't want to reveal itself here, she realized. Of course it wouldn't appear at school in the middle of the afternoon.

It needs to stay safe, so where could it have gone? she thought. *Maybe it's left me a clue to where it's hiding!*

Elodie hurried to the end of the corridor, desperate to find out more, and she slipped quietly out of the nearest door, but the playground was empty. Apart from a scattering of pale gold sand. Elodie looked around. Sure enough, at the far end of the playground, just before the school gates, there was a bigger pile of sand – and stamped in it was a single peculiar footprint. It was unlike anything she'd ever seen before. The print was hoof-shaped yet the mark it left looked more like a seashell. Before she could study it for any longer, the wind stirred the sand and the footprint disappeared.

Not wanting to waste any more time, Elodie rushed to fetch the pencils for art and tried her best to sketch what she'd seen – it was all she could think about. When, at last, the school day came to an end, she rushed back to the playground to look for more footprints. But there was no sign that there'd been any sand there at all.

"Hey!" cried Marnie-Mae as she walked towards the school gates with their unicorn-seeking friend Rishi at Oak Grove garden. "Don't forget we're meeting Kit and Caleb."

Elodie nodded brightly. She was about to tell them about what she'd seen when Marnie started speaking again, her words tumbling out in a rush.

"So snuck on to the blog during IT class and saw a few bizarre reports of unicorn shadows, but I don't know if any of them are real." Marnie pulled out her notes. "Listen to this… *Greetings, Unicorn Seekers, from sunny Mexico! We don't know if we're being visited by a unicorn or a ghost! Every night, my poor children are woken up by whinnies and snorts, and the merry stomping of hooves, but all we ever see is a creature in shadow form! It's very intriguing and a little bit spooky – any thoughts?*

"Then there's another guy in East London," Marnie continued, "who runs a cheese shop. He says: *Hey, seekers – awesome to be in touch! This might sound wild but I think a unicorn is hanging out in my cheese cellar! I've heard it, I swear! I noticed all the cheese it's been gobbling up, and I've even got close to seeing it – but so far only spotted its shadow.*

"And a woman who owns a hotel near Lake

Garda left this message: *Ciao, my London friends, from beautiful Italy – I am lucky enough to know an entire glory of unicorns who visit every summer, splashing gracefully at the edge of the lake. They only appeared in shadow form at first, but then slowly emerged over time, once they were certain they had my trust. I cherish seeing them – it truly is a form of magic."*

"Have you guys found another unicorn?" gasped Rishi. He was still in a state of awe from learning that unicorns were even real. It was Rishi who'd discovered Dash, Stormy's dad, behind his recycling bins last autumn.

"Yes … almost," Elodie said a little uncertainly. "I think it's been trying to reach me all day – I've only seen its shadow though," she explained.

At that moment, Kit and Caleb skated over to join them. Behind the brothers was a rather hot-looking Rufus with their mum, Sophia.

"Tell me everything!" said Rishi as they all set off together, making their way to the Oak Grove estate, where he lived. They were meeting his mum in the community garden.

Elodie recounted her day and then Marnie shared

her findings from the blog.

Kit was captivated, and he even managed to take notes as he glided smoothly along. Rishi practically inhaled every detail, excitement lighting up his smile. Caleb listened too, gazing down as he skated, soothed by the familiar rhythm of his blades.

His friends understood that he didn't have to look at them to be listening, which was a relief to Caleb. He found it much easier to listen to his friends if he didn't have to also engage. It gave him the space to process everything and respond when he was ready. So he said nothing about the beautiful beachy dreams he'd been having, or the wild sandy unicorn who roamed through them. When they reached the gentle shade of the community garden, he settled down beside Rufus beneath the golden-brown pear tree and waited for a nice cool drink.

Rishi's mum, Anisha, was seated comfortably on her meditation cushion, with two warm chai lattes in her hands, waiting for Sophia. She grinned at them all with a warm joy.

"How's the secret Unicorn Seekers' Society doing?" she asked.

"We're good, thanks," said Marnie-Mae politely, throwing a quick wink to her friends, so none of them would give away that they'd almost discovered another one.

The mums were all pretty cool and had been part of the rescue mission for Stormy, Dash and Lumi. But there was no point in involving them too soon. It took away from the fun, mystery and magic of discovering unicorns themselves.

As Anisha and Sophia talked about an upcoming yoga retreat they were planning to run together, the five friends and one big dog got comfy.

"This is the hoofprint I found in the playground," said Elodie, trying to finish her drawing, though it was a little rushed and still not quite right.

Caleb studied it for a moment. "I've seen those in the park," he stated.

"Really? Where?" Rishi asked, wide-eyed with excitement.

"All over," Caleb informed them. "And in my dreams."

"In your dreams?" echoed Elodie, feeling the stirrings of a discovery.

"Yes," replied Caleb. "They're the hoofprints of the beach unicorn that charges through my dreams all night."

"Is that why you've been waking up a lot?" asked Kit.

Caleb nodded and then folded in on himself, suddenly looking deeply worried.

"What's bothering you?" asked Marnie-Mae. She crouched down next to him to comfort him without touching, just the way he liked.

"Bad things," he mumbled, shaking his head.

"In the dream?" said Elodie, whisper-soft, and Caleb nodded.

"This must be the same unicorn I saw at school, and the one we heard in the maze," said Elodie. "It needs us," she concluded. "Don't worry, Caleb – we'll find wherever it's hiding and help it to get home. Can you tell us which glory you think it's from?"

"Surf Dancer," replied Caleb without missing a beat. "She's sandy coloured, with pale grey eyes and hooves as pink as seashells. Sometimes I can just make out her pink horn and sea-foam mane."

"Oh, she's not a shadow to you?" exclaimed Kit. "You've actually *seen* her?"

Caleb shrugged to indicate that, yes, sometimes he had.

"The thing I can't figure out," pondered Marnie-Mae, "is where there could be a beach around here? Like, where's the sand coming from?"

They were all quiet for a moment, thinking this through, then Rishi suddenly laughed.

"What if it's not an actual beach? What if it was more of a massive *sandpit*?"

They all stared at each other eagerly, yelling in unison: "The beach-volleyball courts!"

"We only skate past them every day!" cried Kit, rolling his eyes at how obvious it was.

"Let's meet there at twilight," said Elodie, feeling suddenly hopeful.

And so, as the wind stirred the leaves of the pear tree and Rufus licked Caleb's face, the Unicorn Seekers of South London made a plan.

CHAPTER FOUR
SUMMERTIME TWILIGHT

As twilight fell across the lovely leafy park, the five friends and their St Bernard dog, who was ready for a nap, met up at the sports centre. Now experienced unicorn seekers, they'd also made sure to bring gluten-free muffins too.

"We're definitely in the right place," said Rishi as he studied the notes he'd made from his mum's computer and the Palace of Crystal information forum. "Lots of people have seen the shell prints. Also, everyone loves your dad's coffee van, Elle!" he added with a grin.

The entrance was bustling with business on the beautiful summer's evening. Folk were coming and going from basketball practice or swimming lessons.

Among them were a stream of smiling people dressed in vibrant colours and fluorescent flip-flops, speaking in different languages and accents, all rushing to the huge sandy beach-volleyball courts.

The courts were in an enormous outdoor space on the very lowest level of the sports centre. You could gaze down at them from the long concrete strip where Elodie and her friends had all learned to skate. On the soft white sand of the artificial beach, people hugged, laughed and high-fived as music blared, filling the air with the spirit of summertime. It was so uplifting to watch that, as the five friends peered over the edge of the railings, they couldn't help smiling.

"It looks so fun!" Elodie said, beaming.

"I wish we could join in," gushed Marnie.

"There's no one our age down there. We can't join in with adults," Caleb observed.

Kit sighed. "But we can't really see the sand properly from up here."

"Yeah, there's about a thousand different footprints and none of them look like shells," added Marnie-Mae.

"Let's go down there anyway. Maybe ask about a junior club?" Rishi grinned, feeling a wild sense of delight pull at him.

"Great idea!" announced Caleb, surprising everyone.

Kit blinked in surprise. Caleb sometimes found sand too grainy and itchy, and though he loved all the sea-life at the beach, he often preferred to stay on his towel.

"You sure you want to go down to the sand?" Kit asked.

Caleb nodded and said, "I'll just wear my socks."

"Great," said Kit. "You, Elle and Rishi go down. Me and Marnie can stay with Rufus."

"No way!" protested Marnie-Mae. "Let's all go – besides, there's a little dog down there in the sand already."

They stared at where she was pointing and, sure enough, there was a small fox-coloured hound with floppy ears, sandy paws and an adorable little face. It was next to a tall friendly-looking guy in reflective sunglasses. Every time he moved to demonstrate how to throw or hit the ball, the little dog followed, yapping round his ankles, almost tripping him up. It was really quite funny.

"I've got an idea," said Rishi, ruffling Rufus's ears. "Come with me."

Everyone followed Rishi to the lower level, gliding down the sloping pathways. When they got to the fake beach, they took their skates off and stepped through the gate on to the wooden decking in front of the deep golden sand.

All around them was the warmth of the last sunshine of the day.

"If I was a Surf Dancer, this is exactly where I'd hang out," whispered Kit.

"Me too," agreed Rishi.

"Only there's no actual surf," chimed in Marnie-Mae.

"Surf Dancers can live anywhere near sand *and* water," Caleb said gently. "But it doesn't need to be seawater."

"Really?" asked Elodie, looking intrigued. "I thought they were always coastal."

"They were." Caleb shrugged. "But they've adapted."

"Maybe this surfy unicorn likes our lake, just

like Stormy did," whispered Marnie-Mae as the tall friendly-looking guy came over, the little fox-coloured dog proudly accompanying him.

"Hi, are you here for the junior training?" he asked, giving them a broad smile.

"Yes!" cried Marnie-Mae without hesitating.

"Sure," added Kit.

Elodie grinned. "Absolutely."

"Nope," said Caleb firmly.

"Sounds fun," Rishi said.

"You've just missed it today," the man told them. "But you can come back for a free trial tomorrow. And if you sign up you even get a club T-shirt."

As he spoke, Elodie saw the courts reflected in his mirrored sunglasses. The summery sand, the colourful players and there, just at the edge near the fence, she caught a glimpse of a little horse. Her heart raced, her hair softly crackled, and her feet spun her round so she was staring at the exact spot where the unicorn had been. But, of course, it had cleverly vanished.

Rufus, who had been lingering beside Caleb at the back of the group, chose this moment to amble forward and make friends with the little bright-eyed dog.

The tall guy seemed quite charmed by Rufus, but gave them an apologetic shrug.

"No dogs on the sand, I'm afraid. Even Luna's not really meant to join in," he said, gesturing to the cute dog.

"That's fine," said Rishi. "We're very good at looking after dogs. Maybe we could offer you our very professional dog-sitting services." With that, he gave Luna a little pat.

Everyone turned to stare at him in surprise.

"Our *what now*?" whispered Marnie, looking confused.

"We're keen dog-walkers," said Rishi confidently, "and we're always in this park. We can look after your little dog – Luna, was it? – right now if you like?"

The guy was silent for a moment, clearly considering Rishi's offer.

"I mean that would be super helpful," he said. "And Luna loves making new friends. If you could just keep her off the sand for me for the next hour, that would be great."

The Unicorn Seekers all smiled and nodded enthusiastically.

"How much do you charge?" asked the guy, giving them a warm grin.

"We'll do it for a free T-shirt each," answered Rishi. And so it was settled.

As Kit, Rishi and Marnie-Mae played games with Rufus and the rather delightful Luna, Elodie and Caleb got to work searching for signs of their surf-dancing unicorn.

It didn't take long for Caleb to discover more prints. After he'd reluctantly slipped his blades off, he found they were everywhere, muddled in with the delicate imprint of magpie claws, foxes' prints and little paw marks from Luna.

"They don't seem to lead anywhere though," he said with a sigh.

"What about in there?" suggested Elodie, gesturing to a wooden beach hut that looked like it was part changing room, part storage space, part hang-out lounge for the players.

Stealthily, they crept inside. It was musty and dark, but unexpectedly soothing.

The perfect place to have a nap, thought Caleb, who was still quite tired from the wild unicorn dreams that were disturbing his sleep. He glanced around, looking for somewhere soft to sit down. There was a little desk in one corner, a glass-fronted fridge full of green juice and an old, rather sandy leather sofa.

"If I was a unicorn, I'd definitely have a snooze on there," he muttered, more to himself than Elodie.

"Me too," she said, sinking on to the squishy sofa. At once, her hair tingled with tiny bolts of blue lightning.

As Elodie's eyes widened with hope, Caleb put a finger to his lips.

"Listen," he whispered.

Elodie sat in trembling silence. And sure enough, soft as breath, they heard the tiniest, faintest little snort.

She shot to her feet and together they peered behind the sofa, gripping each other's hands in amazement. For there, in the deep, dreamy dark, was a beautiful, sleeping Surf Dancer, her crystalline horn glimmering sharp as bone.

The two friends stared in wide-eyed astonishment.

"Should we wake her?" whispered Elodie, but she already knew the answer. It would be chaos if they disturbed the little unicorn now. There was no way they could get her past the sandy courts without being spotted, and what if she went wild and charged at someone?

Caleb tilted his head to one side for a long moment, considering what to do.

"She's always reaching me in my dreams, so maybe we can reach her in hers. You did it with Dash – do you think you could try again? Ask her to find you, or see what's wrong?"

Elodie nodded. She sat back down on the sofa and closed her eyes. She had only done this a few times before and it took a lot of love and focus.

At first, she sensed nothing but the sandy dark of the beach hut and the rhythm of the Surf Dancer's smooth little snores, and then at the edge of her mind, like the glow of a new star, she felt the unicorn's tumbling thoughts.

The Surf Dancer was running, racing over wide, sweeping sand dunes, then down to the silver waves of the sea. In the vision, as Elodie dipped her toes into the water, she was amazed to find that the waves were as warm as a bath.

Beside her, the merry unicorn splashed and danced. Elodie reached out to touch her sea-foam mane, but the creature bolted, speeding towards a little strip of restaurants and seaside hotels.

Elodie got the swift sense that she was supposed to follow, yet she couldn't keep up. Running in the sand was tricky. The last thing she saw was the unicorn vanishing into the courtyard of a hotel called Views of Venice before the sound of a whistle brought her back to the beach hut.

Blinking, she adjusted her sight to the gloom of the hut. Caleb had his hands over his ears and looked quite cross.

Elodie smiled at him reassuringly and said, "I think the whistle just means training's over – we'd better get back to the others."

"Did you reach the unicorn?" he asked.

Elodie shook her head. "Not quite. But let's leave a trail of gluten-free muffin crumbs. Maybe she'll follow them."

Caleb cheered up at once. He scattered blueberry muffin crumbs – a known unicorn favourite – behind him as the five Unicorn Seekers left the beach-volleyball courts together and made their way to Elodie's flat for tea.

From Araminta Lang to Elyse de Lyon

October 17th 1918, Venice, Italy

Dearest Elyse,

As you and I both know, for as long as there have been dreams and thunder, there have been unicorns. Through my countless adventures and many far-flung travels, when I've seen wild horses dance beneath a desert moon or vanish beneath the waves of a star-kissed sea, I always sensed something magical was unfolding.

After glimpsing a unicorn in my childhood, I carried a quiet belief in enchantment. But it wasn't until I encountered my beautiful Athena on the beaches close to Venice that I knew the legends were real.

She was like nothing I'd ever witnessed before: a mythical miracle come true.

At first, I thought she was a regular sand-coloured horse, trotting merrily through the surf. But as she drew nearer, and the dawn began to break, I noticed her hooves were the pale pink of seashells, her mane the colour of sea foam, her eyes pale grey like mermaid scales. And then, as the waves softly broke, I caught the glimmer of a bone-sharp horn.

Over time, I was lucky enough to befriend her; she even let me sketch and study her. I've learned from the book of drawings belonging to Princess Grace that there are many different types of unicorns, who run in herds called glories. From studying her sketches, I've learned that the unicorns in Athena's glory are known as Surf Dancers.

I've had a wonderful summer with Athena, but now I am growing gravely concerned for her safety. Some of the friendly locals know of the unicorns who visit this beach and are very protective of them, guarding their secret existence over many years. However, I have heard terrible rumours that this is not the case everywhere.

Indeed, it is said that in Venice the Venetia House of Handbags are befriending a unicorn for all the wrong reasons.

I ask for your assistance in how I might keep Athena hidden...

Much love,
Araminta

P.S. I have sent along a copy of Princess Grace's sketches for your enjoyment. You can see the Surf Dancers in there too.

A FINE DAY IN MAY

1500s. Gardens of the Palace of Crystal

**Burning Sand Spells:
Desert unicorns**
Sandy in colour with creamy
manes, shire-horse hooves
and white horns.

**Nightingale's Heart:
Forest unicorns**
Deep chestnut-brown coats,
reddish manes, mossy green
hooves and amber horns.

**Twilight Grace:
Mist/Rain unicorns**
Grey, silver or white unicorns,
with lilac manes and irises.

**Juniper Blue:
Valley unicorns**
Often multicoloured,
but with blue horns.

From the sketchbook of the Royal Princess Grace,
aged 11, listing the different types of unicorn.

Winter's Dawn:
Snow and Ice unicorns
Entirely white with glassy
horns, frost-blue manes,
tails and hooves.

Surf Dancer:
Beach unicorns
Golden or pale brown, with
shell-pink hooves and horns,
and sea-foam manes.

Indigo River:
Water unicorns
Deepest black, indigo
mane, clear, ice-like horn
and hooves.

Cloud-spun Dreamer:
Mountain unicorns
White or grey, clumpy
hooves and wings!

CHAPTER FIVE

THE MIDNIGHT GATHERING

Something woke Elodie, pulling her sharply from the depths of her dream.

She sat up at once, alert. Her hair crackled as she peered between her bedroom curtains. Moonlight bathed the streets in silver, but the road beneath her window was empty, apart from Pirate the cat, who was prowling like a hunter, searching keenly for mice.

Elodie let her eyes drift to the treeline of the park opposite, watching as the breeze swayed the blossom-filled branches, their leafy shadows dancing in the light of the moon. There was no sign, though, of the Surf Dancer she'd discovered with Caleb.

Around her, the flat was silent and dark, her

parents sound asleep. She threw on her slippers and polka-dot dressing gown and crept into the lounge where the curtains had been left wide open. Maman never closed them – just in case a unicorn ever came galloping by, needing their help.

Elodie settled herself on the sofa, tucking her legs beneath her as she gazed at the night sky. Would the blueberry muffin crumbs be enough? Would the young unicorn be able to find her? Perhaps she ought to go back to sleep. Wait to see if the little Surf Dancer might reach her through her dreams.

The wind gently rattled the windows. Then the silence was broken by an alarmed screech from Pirate. Elodie leapt up and stared out of the window, her hair a mass of gleaming blue with lightning.

Somewhere in the flat came the sound of Maman stirring. But Elodie hardly heard her – she was so focused on the clatter of hooves, the hopeful pounding of her heart, the sense that something wild and unstoppable was rushing towards her.

Suddenly the night was full of starlight, the air filled with salt, slipping through every open window, crack and the space beneath the door.

Maman stepped into the room, her eyes wide, her hands pressed to her chest in anticipation. But Elodie rushed past her, out of the flat, down the stairs and through the bright blue front door into the starry, salt-struck street.

The night was full of sea-kissed magic. A whinny sounded wildly on the wind, loud as the call of a gull, and Elodie peered down the street, her heart racing. From between the trees, she spied the fierce glint of a crystalline horn and a horse-shaped shadow slinking through the night, its hooves kicking up sand.

The little shadow stopped still as a statue, devouring something on the ground before lurching forward at a terrific speed.

The trail of crumbs worked! Elodie thought with a sigh of relief.

The unicorn darted wildly back and forth across the road, clearly searching for more crumbs. She seemed to be coming closer to her flat. Elodie stepped back, a little stunned, astonished by the creature's sea-swept majesty.

The Surf Dancer was the colour of golden sand, with a mane of glittering sea foam and hooves of shell pink. She looked so much fiercer now that she was awake – Elodie could hardly believe it was the same unicorn.

Her pink horn glinted dangerously in the moonlight, as she hungrily gobbled up the crumbs. She raised her head and her sea-grey eyes met Elodie's. They were wild as the waves and completely untamed.

Gently, Elodie held out her arms in greeting. The unicorn pawed the ground with her hoof, reminding Elodie of a bull about to charge. She was fearless – her rushing energy as deep and magnificent as an uncharted ocean. The creature held her gaze. Elodie kept still – and the unicorn bolted.

Straight towards Elodie.

At the very last moment, Elodie hurled herself into a nearby hedge as the unicorn streaked past her, into her building, and pounded up the stairs. Without hesitation, Elodie gave chase.

The door to the Singhs' flat creaked open and Mrs Singh peered out, giving Elodie a small grin.

"You've found another one, you clever girl!" she said before quickly closing the door.

Elodie barely had a chance to respond – it seemed that this unicorn was starving and brimming with mischief.

Less than a minute later, Elodie was back in the flat – and found Maman perched on the sofa, sipping a large mug of organic oat-milk coffee, while the unicorn was busily munching a baguette!

"She's just a little hungry," Maman explained as Elodie's dad set a small bowl of hot chocolate down for the Surf Dancer to drink.

The scent of lavender, apricots and freshly made croissants drifted from the kitchen and Elodie realized her dad was already baking, which was confusing. The clock in the hallway showed that it had only just turned midnight; they had hours until sunrise.

What was going on?

Elodie was about to ask him, but he'd slipped out of the room, speaking on the phone in a low voice.

That's odd, she thought. She would not have been surprised if Maman had called one of her unicorn-seeker networks at the Ministry of Magical Creatures to ask for help, but it was strange that her dad would

be on the phone to anyone in the middle of the night.

Suddenly the unicorn stamped her shell-shaped hoof and Elodie tried not to jump.

Maman calmly put her coffee down and stood up, very gently laying a hand upon the unicorn's nose. The little creature shook her head indignantly, scattering sand everywhere. Elodie could only watch in wonder.

Maman remained calm as the Surf Dancer pranced curiously round the lounge, her horn snagging on the curtains, the whip of her tail almost spilling the mug of coffee, her small nose knocking over a vase of water, as well as the entire bouquet of lilies that were neatly arranged in it. Eventually, though, the little unicorn stretched out on the sunflower rug, chewing contentedly on a few lilies, her horn luminescent as starlight, her wild grey eyes staring around the room.

Silently and carefully, Elodie knelt beside her.

And there they stayed for some moments until the dazzling unicorn turned her beautiful face to Elodie, blinking slowly. As Elodie gazed at the magnificent creature, a name came to her – whispered as softly as the threads of a dream.

Skylar.

It made Elodie think of endless summer, cottony white clouds and sapphire-blue seas – it was perfect. Magically, the entire lounge was now dusted in sand, as if Skylar had brought the beach indoors.

Outside, from the street below, there came the sound of a car pulling up, followed by a light knock on the front door downstairs.

"What's going on?" asked Elodie in a mild daze as her dad went to answer the main door.

Maman winked at her. "It's time for the Unicorn Seekers of South London to assemble," she said, smiling. "Your dad called everyone and they're on their way."

Elodie blinked in amazement. They'd never had a midnight meeting before. This felt special and urgent.

"Is Skylar in danger?" she whispered, fear seeping into her voice.

Maman frowned. "I'm afraid that she might be. I've heard whispers through my network of a Surf Dancer running through Europe, trying to escape a grave fate. There must be a reason she sought you out. It's your duty to protect her, Elle."

Maman drew an old weather-beaten letter from her dressing-gown pocket and handed it to Elodie.

It looked like an ancient treasure, as fragile as stardust. Elodie was about to unfold it when she heard Marnie-Mae and her mum, Joni, coming rather noisily up the stairs.

"So this is the Surf Dancer!" cried Marnie-Mae, rushing into the lounge and leaping on to the sofa. She was in pyjamas and bright pink sequin trainers.

Skylar shook out her mane but stared at Marnie-Mae and Joni a little warily.

"Still looks like a horse to me," said Joni with a shrug. She was wrapped in a rather marvellous floral robe that was more like something you'd wear to a wedding than a dressing gown. The neat dark coils of her hair were hidden beneath an elegant bright yellow silk wrap. And she had lipstick on … at midnight!

"Well, Mum," explained Marnie, "this is the unicorn we've got to rescue. She's a Surf Dancer so she needs to be near water and sand."

"Like *in* the sea?" asked Joni, running her eyes over Skylar.

"No, more like at the beach," said Maman.

Joni grinned. "A lady after my own heart."

"But which beach will you take her to? One in Cornwall? Or Dubai? Or maybe Australia or Jamaica?" Marnie asked impatiently.

"We should start with Italy," said a soft, tired voice.

It was Caleb at the door to the flat. With him were Kit, Sophia and Rufus. They were followed closely by Rishi and his mum, who just about fitted into the overcrowded lounge.

The unicorn raised her graceful head, assessing them with sparkling intrigue. A moment of hush swept through the room as the Unicorn Seekers and their families gazed in awe at Skylar. To some she was a bright-eyed horse, but to the Unicorn Seekers her shell-pink horn, which glimmered and shone like sea-light, was magnificent.

Skylar looked at each of them in turn, her wild grey eyes gleaming. Then she gave a little snort and shake of her head, spraying everyone lightly with salt and sand.

"Thank you for all coming," said Maman at last, as Max passed around a tray of hot chocolate and apricot croissants, and a blueberry muffin for Caleb – who was now lingering in the corridor, where there was more space and not so many smells or loud breathing. "As you can see, this little unicorn seems to have got lost and we want to help her find her glory before she draws unwanted attention."

"She belongs in Italy – I know that from my dreams," called Caleb from the corridor, but he sounded nervous, unsure of something.

"I think Caleb's right," Maman agreed, and Elodie nodded, remembering when she'd entered Skylar's dream at the beach hut.

"Elodie, why don't you read out the letter?" said Maman. "I found it in the loft, with your great-grandmother Elyse's things."

Elodie carefully unfolded the letter and began reading the aged, faded note from Araminta Lang.

When she finished, everyone looked deep in thought, not quite sure what to make of it. Rufus gave a little woof and Caleb shuffled into the doorway.

"That House of Handbags was in one of my dreams," he told them. "There's a unicorn there that's in trouble … some sort of terrible danger. I think Skylar came here to find us because she needs our help to protect her family."

The Unicorn Seekers and their families stared at each other. One thing was settled: they were heading to Venice!

"We've actually got a trip to Italy planned," Sophia said, smiling. "We could set off early. Swing through Venice first, before Milan."

Elodie's parents exchanged a glance, then gave Elodie a sad smile.

"It's the Palace of Crystal Annual Fair next week," said her dad. "I'm supplying all the coffees, so I won't be able to make it."

Elodie blinked in shock. "Maman, you can drive the van though?"

"I'm afraid I'll have to stay and help your dad," said Esme, gently squeezing Elodie's hand. "But I know you Unicorn Seekers are fully capable of handling this adventure."

"B-but…" Elodie stammered, "how will we get there?"

"If there's any sort of handbags involved, you can

count me in!" piped up Joni. "We can go by train, bring that little horse with us."

"Mum, she's a unicorn called Skylar!" cried Marnie-Mae, rolling her eyes.

"We can't go either," said Rishi with a long sigh. "Our cousins are coming from Delhi. I can't wait to see them, but I'm sad to miss the adventure."

"You can keep an eye on everything here," said Kit reassuringly. "Make sure no other Surf Dancers turn up."

Rishi beamed at this. "Yeah, I could keep looking after Luna and hang out at the beach-volleyball courts – my cousins would love that."

So, as Skylar shook out her sea-foam mane and the stars twinkled in the midnight sky, hot chocolate was sipped, secrets were whispered and a trip to Italy was planned.

And it would begin the very next morning.

CHAPTER SIX
SECRET OF THE SURF DANCERS

At six minutes to sunrise, as the last of the stars twinkled out over the London sky, Elodie, Max and Esme tiptoed into the lovely leafy park. The little unicorn pranced round them, light-footed as a deer. They came to a stop at the Feather and Fern coffee van.

"Are you sure you'll be OK?" asked Esme, tenderly stroking a crackle of lightning from Elodie's curls. Elodie nodded and hugged her parents close, aware of Skylar happily trampling the last of the spring bluebells and munching thistles behind her.

"I'll be fine," she assured them, feeling the bittersweet excitement of having a unicorn adventure without her parents.

A friendly bark rang through the air and Elodie grinned as Rufus came bounding over eagerly, followed by Caleb, Kit and Sophia, all looking keen to get things moving. Elodie's eyes darted to Caleb, but he was staring at the ground, deep in thought or lost in worry. It was difficult to know.

Perhaps he felt the same responsibility of being one of the lead seekers as much as Elodie did. Though it was wildly exciting, it meant everything was down to them.

"Good morning!" called Joni, strutting up to the Feather and Fern, dressed in a rather wonderful sarong, colourful T-shirt, a huge sun hat, enormous sunglasses and gold sandals, with a jacket thrown over her shoulders.

"Who's ready to get this Surf Dancer back to the beach?" cried Marnie-Mae, pulling Elodie into a hug.

"I'm just going to do a quick sunrise stretch," said Sophia, unrolling her yoga mat. "Then we'll head straight for the airport. The boys have got their passports ready."

"So we'll meet you in St Mark's Square in

Venice!" Joni said, beaming.

"Do you think Skylar will be OK on the trains?" asked Kit with an anxious shrug.

"Surf Dancers are a very well-adapted glory," Esme explained. "They've had to live close to people for a long time as there is hardly any shelter on beaches. I'm sure Skylar will have some undiscovered skills that even I don't know about."

The bright-eyed group of friends nodded, taking in Esme's words.

"Here are some snacks for the journey," said Max, handing Elodie a box crammed with delicious-looking gluten-free pastries and a big flask of decaf coffee to Joni.

"We'll see you soon in Venice," added Kit, high-fiving his friends.

Maman laid a rose-scented kiss on Elodie's forehead, and Max gave her one last big hug.

Caleb walked quietly over to Skylar and bowed his head to her as a sign of respect. The sandy unicorn softly nuzzled his hair with her nose and gave a happy neigh, before scampering off after Elodie, Marnie and Joni, up the little hill towards the station.

Elodie gripped the box of treats with one hand and, with the other, waved to her parents, trying her best to ignore the sharp pain of saying goodbye. It was a great honour to be trusted with the task of rescuing a unicorn, and it wasn't as if they hadn't done it before. Even so, Elodie would miss her maman and dad. She gave a little gulp, and Marnie gently squeezed her hand.

"It's cool, Elle – it'll all work out," she said, tucking her braids behind her ears.

Reaching the old Victorian station on the other side of the hill, they found it completely empty and all the ticket gates open as it was so early in the morning.

"You see, girls – this'll be a breeze," said Joni with smile as they sneaked Skylar on to the platform and into the last carriage of the train. A few commuters blinked at them in surprise, but mostly they were ignored. People seemed so busy on their phones and laptops that they simply glanced in surprise but then got back to work.

To Marnie and Elodie's delight, Skylar was quite content on the train, as if she'd done this many times before. She settled down on the floor at their feet like a large golden dog, her shell-pink horn gleaming and her pale grey eyes blinking in the morning sunshine.

As the train rumbled away, Elodie gazed out of the window, watching the leafy park fade away. Skyscrapers and office blocks rolled into view and it felt like no time at all before they arrived at St Pancras station in London.

"Right, girls, stay by my side at all times and pretend this is totally normal!" whispered Joni, raising her sunglasses to give them a secretive wink.

Marnie-Mae's eyes opened wide with delight. "Shall we say we're champion showjumpers on the way to a competition?"

"Or farmers off to a village fair in the French countryside?" added Elodie.

"We'll say we're fabulously rich and this is our most beloved pet who we simply can't travel without," said Joni with a rather marvellous swish of her sun hat.

Elodie and Marnie-Mae scrambled off the train with all their belongings and the box of treats. Skylar obediently followed, trotting elegantly between them, her sea-grey eyes fluttering with curiosity and a trail of silvery sand scattering behind her.

Very few people in the bustling station seemed to notice the mythical creature cantering among them, like the glimmer of a dream. Until…

"Unicorn!" cried a little boy in a pushchair, pointing in delight.

Elodie felt a beat of worry pulse through her heart. But the boy's family were all too busy finding their tickets to pay any attention to him.

As they joined the queue for the Eurostar, Joni applied more lipstick and pulled out a stunning white fan. Elodie laid a hand on Skylar's beautiful mane, trying to sense the unicorn's thoughts, and was amazed to find she was serenely calm.

"Maman was right," she murmured to Marnie. "Surf Dancers are very comfortable around people."

When their turn came, Elodie and Marnie-Mae nervously handed over their tickets and passports to a bright-eyed attendant, a young Parisian woman, who stared at Skylar with amusement.

"You can't take a baby horse on the Eurostar," she said firmly but pleasantly.

"Firstly, this is an endangered mythical being," Joni replied in a casual tone, fanning herself with the sleek white fan, "and, secondly, we will cover any costs required."

The young attendant laughed, shrugged and shook her head.

Skylar stepped forward and Elodie winced a little, worried that Skylar's horn might accidentally strike the attendant in the face. Instead, the young woman stopped laughing and stared at Skylar in awe and disbelief, her mouth falling open.

"But that's… It's not… It's impossible," she stammered.

Elodie and Marnie-Mae both turned to each other, instantly guessing that this attendant must be a seeker who had forgotten her gift.

"It's clever, isn't it?" said Marnie-Mae, improvising. "You see, we're actually rescuing Skylar from a magical circus," she continued, giving the woman a sparkling grin.

Elodie joined in. "Yes, the circus of illusion. Skylar was their most famous act, but she hated performing. We must get her to Paris so she can be set free."

"Free?" breathed the young woman, as if lost in another world.

"At our chateau," explained Joni airily. "She will be free to roam all the acres and vineyards we own."

"Yes, I see," said the astonished attendant, still half in a daze. "I can let you through, but I've no idea how you'll get on the train…"

"Let us worry about that," Joni replied.

With that, she gave a melodramatic flick of her fan, and they were soon past security and making their way down a long slope towards the Eurostar platform.

A throng of people pressed in round them, gaping and whispering in wonderment, all pointing and staring at Skylar. Joni laid a reassuring hand on Skylar's mane and cut through the crowds as if she truly was a millionaire on her way to an urgent appointment. Elodie and Marnie had to run to keep up.

"The train looks packed," said Elodie as they got ready to board.

"Don't worry, Elle, we'll find a way," Marnie-Mae reassured her, but, as she spoke, Joni let out a very quiet gasp. Elodie and Marnie gripped each other's hands in alarm. Skylar had vanished into thin air!

The two friends stared about in alarm.

"We can't have lost her already," said Elodie, feeling panic rising inside her.

Suddenly Joni breathed an enormous sigh of relief and gestured with her fan to the little horse-shaped shadow beside her.

"She's still with us," she said, chuckling. "Just invisible."

"This is what your mum meant about Surf Dancers!" Marnie-Mae said to Elodie in a rather dramatic stage whisper. "They have *undiscovered skills…* This must be one of them."

Elodie thought back to the times in the maze and playground when Skylar had seemed so incredibly close, but had then seemingly vanished. *She has been close by. She was just invisible.*

"This way, girls," said Joni, following a trail of fine sand on to the Eurostar.

She settled down in her seat to read, while Elodie and Marnie-Mae followed Skylar to the buffet car, where she seemed to want to stay. Her shadow was clearly sniffing at the ice cream.

"Let's try this," Elodie suggested.

She opened the box of treats from her dad and sprinkled a trail of muffin crumbs back to their seats. They didn't have long to wait before they saw the little gluten-free chunks magically disappearing as Skylar gobbled them up.

"Watch out!" cried Marnie-Mae as the invisible creature wriggled on to their laps, lying like a huge dog across them, her horn resting on the window.

They giggled and shared the special look of two best friends with a magical secret.

"This is going to be our best adventure yet," said Elodie.

Even though her parents were back at home, Elodie knew that with the help of her friends, everything would work out OK and they would find Skylar's glory.

As the train set off for the glittering city of Paris, the two friends and the mythical beast snuggled down to sleep.

Hey Marnie, Elle, Caleb and Kit – Rishi here! How's it going? I'm so sorry to be missing the adventure. I've been up all night having chai lattes with Mum and we've found out some great stuff about Surf Dancers. See below!

Barcelona Museum of Enchanted Art

Study 21: A Surf Dancer's hoofprints or, as they're fondly known, a beach dipper. A coastal unicorn that not only dips in and out of the sea, but remains out of sight too. It's as if it hides in the very air – hence there is no actual portrait, just a drawing of an empty beach dotted with seashell hoofprints.

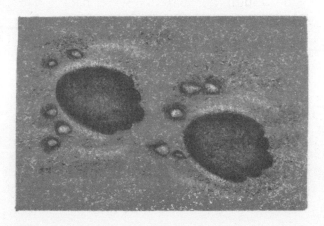

From the University of Southern California,
Department of Enchanted Studies.
Extract from The Observation of
Mythical Beings *by Cintra Sidelle*

It seems that for many decades people have held the fierce belief that anyone can see a unicorn if the weather conditions are right, preferably during a mild storm, and especially if the person is carrying muffins or dandelions. However, when it comes to the beach-dwelling glory Surf Dancers, this does not seem to be the case. They are exceptional at vanishing. Like desert mirages, they slip in and out of thin air.

The Bookshop of Imagined Realities, Rio de Janeiro

Today our monthly book club meeting was an absolute gem! An evening of literature and fiction ... and tales of the impossible. Not only did we drink the best Brazilian coffee in Ipanema, we also discussed our latest favourite read: *I Wish I was a Horse*. We shared our collective stories of seeing an actual sand-coloured pony on Copacabana Beach.

Some of our readers had a beautiful theory that this horse is secretly a unicorn with special powers, including being able disappear into the atmosphere whenever anyone gets too close.

Oh, how I long for this to be true! Another reader suggested we take some cheesecake to the beach to try to tempt 'the horse' to the bookshop! I would love to try this. Not sure my boss would agree though... Anyway, see you next time! The book club is held on the last Tuesday of each month, and maybe the magical horse will be joining us – who knows?

Bianca's Boatyard Cafe, Barbados

Welcome to the best cafe in the Caribbean. We serve rum cake, rum coffee, rum chocolate and many other rum-based delights – along with fresh fish caught right here in the bay, and wholesome plant-based meals from food picked from our own gardens.

We are a little low on apple pies this week, though, because a neighbouring wild horse — AKA Sea Shanty — has been gatecrashing our lunches and stealing apples from the tree in our back garden.

We don't know how he gets away with it as we never manage to catch him, but we know it's him from the seashell hoofprints. The cheeky menace! Ha!

Actually, we're super fond of Sea Shanty, and we're happy to share our sweet food with him any time. We just love it when he pops by on BBQ days to mingle with and charm our customers — and sometimes sample a sip of rum! Some even claim he's enchanted. I don't know about that, but I appreciate that he values Bianca's Boatyard Cafe as the best place on the beach.

Hope this helps your adventures in Venice!
Rishi
P.S. I'm starting beach volleyball tomorrow - I can't wait!

CHAPTER SEVEN
UNICORN DREAMS

Elodie drifted into a deep and stirring dream and found herself on a seashore of soft silvery sand. Behind her were rows of restaurants and cafes all with lovely Italian names, but more stunning were the waves of a glorious turquoise sea lapping the shore. Something about the sway and pull of the water felt exhilarating and she ran straight towards it, laughing with joy.

The moment Elodie's toes touched the waves, she gave a happy sigh, for the salt water was not cool or chilly like in Brighton but warm and welcoming. At once, Elodie plunged in, clothes and all.

A sapphire-blue wave broke over her head and tiny darts of lightning shimmered in her hair.

Suddenly her heart pounded and Elodie stood up in the surf. She turned to face the beach, her eyes searching wildly along the empty shore as the sound of galloping hooves splashed by.

But where was the creature? The beach was deserted. Which meant it had to be a unicorn in hiding.

A Surf Dancer!

Perhaps it's Skylar and she's turned invisible, Elodie thought, cupping her hands and calling the unicorn gently through the soft breeze.

"Skylar! Skylar!"

"It's not Skylar," said a familiar voice.

Elodie blinked in amazement, for there was Caleb standing just before the beach, at the edge of the sand, shielding his eyes from the dazzling sun.

"Caleb!" she cried, waving in delight. "How do you know which unicorn it is?"

"I've seen her," Caleb answered. "She's from Skylar's glory. I think her name is Delphi. She might be Skylar's sister."

The moment Caleb spoke the beautiful name *Delphi*, Elodie felt a change in the current, as if the tide was turning. Her hair began to crackle and the unicorn's hooves came thundering powerfully towards her. For a rare glittering moment, Elodie saw her: a creature just like Skylar but sleeker and faster, her eyes glowing, her horn lethal.

Astonished, Elodie stepped back as the unicorn raced past her towards Caleb. But suddenly he looked worried and started waving his arms in alarm.

"Go back to the sea! Stay off the sand!" Caleb cried anxiously, ducking out of the unicorn's path.

A shout came from further up the beach. Elodie spun round to see a splendidly dressed older gentleman marching forcefully in Caleb's direction, with a lasso made of blue lightning pointing straight at him and the wild unicorn.

Elodie's heart clenched.

"Caleb, run!" she screamed.

And then she was startled awake, her glorious curls zinging with lightning, sand scattering from her skin, her breath caught in her throat.

"What's the matter, Elle?" yelped Marnie-Mae, throwing her arms round Skylar who had woken at the commotion and become fully visible, her tail flicking like an angry cat. Skylar's eyes were wide and darting, and her horn shone fiercely.

Two teenage boys on nearby seats peered over in amusement.

"Neat horse," said one, getting ready to take a photo on his phone.

"No pictures," interrupted Joni. "Skylar's a VIP and so we'll have to charge you a hefty sum for a photograph."

The boys looked confused, but they reluctantly put their phones away, whispering together as they turned back to their comics.

Before Elodie could tell her best friend about the dream, Marnie-Mae gasped, pointing to the notification that had just lit up her mum's phone.

"Rishi messaged us – look!" said Marnie.

As the train zoomed into Paris, the three of them read Rishi's email. He and his mum had found loads of examples of the Surf Dancers' rare ability to stay invisible for great lengths of time. The Surf Dancers were very clever, but also seemed to be the most endangered of the unicorn glories they'd come across so far – people were always coming across them, some not always with the best intentions.

"Wow!" said Marnie. "I can't believe that one in the Caribbean went right up to a cafe and ate with the customers!"

Her mum nodded, but then she noticed Elodie frowning.

"Is everything all right, sweetheart?" Joni asked her gently.

"Yes. No…" Elodie mumbled. "It was my dream. I saw another unicorn from Skylar's glory. Her name was Delphi. Caleb was there too; he thinks Delphi is Skylar's sister. Delphi ran to him but then a man appeared. It was like he had a rope made out of lightning and he was after Delphi. I think she was in grave danger – perhaps that's why Skylar found us. We need to get to Venice as quick as possible."

"We will," Joni assured her. "We're just arriving in Paris. All we have to do is cross the city and catch the overnight train."

"Yeah, but can we at least get some *pains au chocolat* from a real patisserie on the way?" pleaded Marnie, making everyone chuckle. Even Skylar whinnied in agreement.

*

Moving through the arty streets of Paris with a small unicorn was surprisingly easy.

Everyone around them seemed to be in a hurry to get to somewhere fabulous, strutting quickly by in sharp stilettoes or zipping past on scooters, some sipping *chocolat chaud* as they went. Hardly anyone batted an eyelid at a family of three with a beautiful horse.

Being in Paris made Elodie think of her great-grandma, Elyse de Lyon, who had grown up in the French capital and long ago befriended a unicorn called Raven. But, although the joyful buzz of the city and little snippets of French soothed Elodie's soul, reminding her of Maman's lullabies, she still couldn't help feeling wary.

"Paris is where my maman worked for years," she whispered to Marnie-Mae.

"Oh yeah – for the Bureau de Secrets," Marnie whispered back. "We ought to keep a low profile!"

It was never just one person hunting a unicorn. Both friends knew that there were many different networks and organizations all over Europe, particularly in Paris, that wanted to capture one for all the wrong reasons but mostly to use the mythically enchanting power of their horns.

So they rushed past the Eiffel Tower, grabbed all the French pastries they could carry (as their box of snacks had been devoured on the Eurostar) and made their way to the overnight sleeper train to Venice.

"This should do nicely," exclaimed Joni as they entered their own little compartment with four bunk beds – one for each of them, including Skylar.

They waited patiently as Skylar folded herself gracefully on to a bottom bunk. Joni then carefully placed her huge black sunglasses over Skylar's eyes so the unicorn could rest, and delicately arranged a beach towel over her like a blanket.

Marnie-Mae grinned. "She looks super cool."

Elodie nodded. It was true: not only did Skylar look awesome, but she was also partly disguised, so if anyone suspicious glanced into the carriage, they might – in the darkness – mistake her for a horse, a large dog or maybe even a rather eccentric person.

Either way, Elodie felt assured that they were safe, and she closed her eyes, wondering if more strange dreams would haunt her.

But they did not.

When she opened them several hours later, they had arrived in the summery hot city of Venice. The city of masks.

Light streamed in through the windows and the sky was blue and clear.

"I think Skylar should keep your sunglasses, Mum," joked Marnie-Mae as she plaited Skylar's mane. "She looks kind of funny, like a pantomime horse."

Elodie and Joni giggled in agreement. And so Skylar remained in the show-stopping sunglasses as they clambered sleepily off the train.

Around them a wonderful maze of canals sparkled summer blue, flowing through the city and carrying beautiful gondolas and boats full of bright-eyed tourists and people heading to work. Elodie breathed in the scent of sea salt and gelato, her heart skipping with excitement as they set off through the vivid pink sunrise for St Mark's Square.

CHAPTER EIGHT
AN ENCHANTMENT OF HANDBAGS

As they made their way through winding cobblestone streets and over quaint little bridges, Elodie and Marnie both gasped at the sight of hidden alleyways revealing waterside homes whose front doors seemed to open straight on to the canals. Breathtaking architecture surrounded them and little statues of winged lions and sea-swept angels hung off the sides of the buildings. While all around them were the mingling smells of pizza, *espresso* and sun cream.

Skylar at once took the lead, sometimes trotting, sometimes galloping, so the seekers had to sprint to keep up.

"She's definitely from around here," said Joni, clinging on to her hat.

"I want to live in Venice!" cried Marnie-Mae, her violet braids fluttering behind her as she rushed past stalls selling elaborate sequin masks and tiny glass ornaments that glittered in the early-morning sunshine.

"Mum, please can we move here?" she begged.

"I wish we could!" called Joni, dashing to keep up.

Turning away from a little harbour where the bigger boats were docking, they found themselves in a cool, shady street lined with exquisite designer shops selling fabulous Italian clothes, shoes and bags – all hand-crafted in Venice.

Joni came to an abrupt halt in front of a glorious handbag shop with dazzlingly high windows and an exceedingly grand entrance that was decorated with real gold roses arching over the open doorway. It was the most enchanting shop on the street.

"Girls, I have to go in!" Joni pressed her face up against the glass, as if in a trance.

"We haven't really got time for shopping, Mum," said Marnie-Mae with a frown, keeping an eye on the beautiful unicorn prancing anxiously back and forth along the street.

But Joni didn't appear to have heard. She was completely taken with a wonderful large blue leather tote bag, which had a gleaming silver buckle.

Skylar trotted up to the window and peered at the display. Then she began to back away, her eyes glowing strangely behind the huge sunglasses, her horn glinting sharply.

Like a bolt of lightning, Elodie felt the unicorn's fear. She squeezed her eyes closed and sent her thoughts to the surf-dancing creature.

It's all right – stay calm. We'll protect you.

"Skylar's frightened," she whispered to Marnie-Mae. "She can lead me to St Mark's Square. You stay with your mum and meet us there later."

"OK…" said Marnie a little doubtfully. "Mum, we've got to meet Kit and Caleb soon, so you'll have to catch up on fashion later," said Marnie as Elodie and Skylar darted into a twisting alleyway.

But Joni ignored her daughter altogether and hurried towards the shop's golden-rose entrance. A little girl with a sunny, warm smile and a flowery sundress came skipping out of the door, almost knocking into her.

"Where's your unicorn?" she said in a lilting Italian accent, her face serious and her brown eyes large and inquisitive.

Joni blinked in confusion as if awakening from a long sleep.

"What unicorn?" asked Marnie-Mae casually. She was very well practised at pretending to know nothing.

"The one I saw a moment ago," the girl chirped, dancing round the grand entrance. "She looked just like Grandpa's unicorn – only smaller."

Marnie-Mae gave a nervous grin, and the little girl giggled and spun in a cartwheel. She must have only been about six or seven, with long flowing brown hair, olive skin and a playful glint in her eye.

"Your great-grandfather has a unicorn? That sounds amazing," Marnie-Mae joked, forcing a laugh. "Does he run an enchanted riding school?"

"No," said the girl seriously, but then her face lit up a little mischievously. "He runs a handbag emporium," she whispered gleefully. "And Delphi lives in the handbag warehouse by the beach."

Marnie-Mae's mouth fell open.

Delphi.

Hadn't she heard that name before? Wasn't Delphi the name of the unicorn Elodie had dreamed of? The very unicorn that was in grave danger.

"Where is this warehouse?" she asked coolly, pretending to admire a gorgeous yellow satchel in the shop window. It was the colour of sunshine and the more Marnie-Mae gazed at it the more perfect it seemed. As if it was calling out to her.

That's strange, Marnie thought. She wasn't even particularly fond of the colour yellow.

"The Lido di—" the little girl began when a very glamorous woman, dripping in diamonds and floaty silk scarves, leaned out of the golden-rose entrance.

"Francesca!" she called, frowning at the little girl and beckoning her back inside as she lightly scolded her in Italian.

"Yes, Mama!" The little girl, Francesca, darted back into the shop.

Marnie-Mae looked around for her mum, and

spotted her inside at the till. Joni was just about to buy seven handbags of all different sizes and colours, one for every strand of the rainbow.

"Mum!" she gasped, dashing inside. "You can't spend our entire budget for the trip on bags!"

Joni stared at the collection in her arms and gave a bemused laugh.

"Of course not," she said, handing each glorious handbag back to the shop assistant. She shook her head. "I got completely carried away. Don't know what I was thinking!"

All around them crowds of people were checking out colourful bags and trying on accessories with a look of helpless adoration in their eyes.

A Swiss couple were

choosing matching white gloves for their wedding.

An Australian family were getting a set of identical maroon tote bags.

An elderly Greek man was buying a bright fuchsia clutch bag for each of his six granddaughters.

But the moment Marnie-Mae said the word "budget", it seemed the spell was broken. The Swiss couple hastily put the gloves back and left. The Australian family laughed out loud at the absurd idea of having matching bags. And the Greek gentleman yelped in horror at the price before putting everything back and rushing out of the shop.

Marnie-Mae took her mum's hand and led her quickly out of the shop, wondering why on earth the customers were acting so strangely.

"We need to meet up with Elle and the others as soon as possible. Whoever owns that shop also knows where the endangered unicorn is hiding."

The moment they reached St Mark's Square, Skylar was easy to spot, despite the crowds, her mane dazzling in the sunlight. She was standing in the shade of a long stone archway to the left of a magnificent cathedral.

As they dashed towards the bright-eyed Surf Dancer, Marnie-Mae noticed that Elodie had her arms wrapped round the unicorn's sleek neck, as if to calm her. Sitting beside them, on a travel yoga mat, were Caleb, Kit and a dozing Rufus.

"You made it!" cried Marnie, high-fiving her two friends.

Kit leapt up in excitement. "We certainly did!"

"Rufus didn't really like the plane though," Caleb informed them. "He was too squashed. And the food was terrible."

"Well, now you're in Italy I'm sure the food will be delicious," Joni said encouragingly.

"I've got loads to tell you guys," Marnie-Mae blurted out, hopping from foot to foot. And she poured out every detail to her friends.

How Joni became enchanted by a handbag.

How they'd met a curious little girl called Francesca who had Unicorn Sight.

How Francesca's great-grandfather had a warehouse by the beach where a unicorn lived.

How the mysterious unicorn was called Delphi.

"That was the name from my dream," Elodie breathed.

She crouched down low to speak with Caleb, who was still sitting cross-legged on the yoga mat, stroking Rufus's floppy ears.

"Caleb … you were in my dream too, on the beach, with the cross old man who was very smartly dressed."

Caleb kept his eyes on Rufus. He'd also not enjoyed the flight and really wanted breakfast.

"You've been in my dreams too," he said a little grumpily, wishing that Venice wasn't so busy and hot.

"Do you think it was the same dream?" suggested Kit, pulling a pencil from behind his ear and taking notes in his notebook – purposefully plain so no one suspected anything.

"Yes," said Caleb, sounding very certain.

"So who is the man with the lightning lasso?" asked Elodie as Skylar tossed her head from side to side – still a little agitated – almost knocking Joni's sunglasses off the end of her nose.

But Caleb just shrugged. He had no idea.

"What if he's Francesca's great-grandfather?" whispered Marnie-Mae, looking worried.

"We'll have to talk to her. Try and find out where that warehouse is," piped up Kit.

"Well, I certainly can't go in that shop again. It completely bewitched me," said Joni, just as Sophia approached with an armful of sweet-scented, multicoloured ice creams in biscotti cones – perfect for breakfast!

"Italian gelato," she announced, handing out cornets of black cherry, honeycomb, fresh mango, mint-choc-chip and creamy vanilla.

"Guess what, Mum?" Kit grinned. "After breakfast, we're going shopping."

Joni's phone pinged and she peered at the message.

"Elle, it's from your mum. Looks like something unicorn-related."

From Elyse de Lyon to Araminta Lang

March 3rd 1919, Paris, France

Most precious Araminta,

How simply lovely to hear from you and how lucky I am to have someone as well travelled and knowledgeable as you to share my unicorn lore with.

I was so excited when Maman gave me this letter, I rushed straight to the lakeside to read it.

Thank you for telling me about Athena — she sounds enchantingly beautiful. I've spoken with my maman and papa, and, though they themselves aren't seekers, they have managed to get in touch with a family in Venice who are: the Speranzas.

Papa advises you to make contact at once, for your beloved unicorn could be in grave danger.

The Speranza family know of the famed Venetia House of Handbags, and they have heard dark rumours that the company has a long-standing tradition of using the dust of a unicorn's horn for enchantments of a hypnotic nature.

As I'm sure you know, many of my childhood summers were spent with my beautiful Raven, an Indigo River whom I befriended by the Lycée Saint-Charles.

She gave her life protecting me when I turned twenty-one and, though I was devastated to lose her, Raven entrusted her horn to me, to guard its magical properties.

Its powers of enchantment could be used for any number of impossible things: from cloud cutting to being sprinkled over soup to make you look younger; from curing sickness to foretelling the future.

I have kept the remnants of Raven's horn safely hidden in a special lotion inside a tin marked by a winged horse. I never leaves my side wherever I go, so it doesn't fall into the wrong hands.

A well-attended masquerade ball is fast approaching, the Ball of Floating Stars, and you will find the Speranza family in attendance.

All my love,

Your devoted goddaughter, Elyse

CHAPTER NINE

THE MYSTERIOUSLY MAGICAL HANDBAG SHOP

"That's the name of the shop!" Marnie-Mae gasped. "I'm sure of it."

"The Venetia House of Handbags?" said Elodie.

"The place where I got bewitched?" whispered Joni, glancing a little anxiously at Skylar. Sensing her unease, the Surf Dancer stamped her foot. Elodie felt her heart tremble and wrapped her arms more tightly round the beautiful unicorn's neck.

Caleb stared up from the yoga mat with a look of dismay, gripping his mint-choc-chip ice cream in horror.

"I think the owners of the shop are going to use Delphi's horn to enchant more of their handbags," he breathed.

Sophia turned quite pale, while everyone else looked aghast.

"So that means that they'll grind up Delphi's horn into magic dust or something?"

"Not If we get to her first," said Kit decisively, and they all nodded.

"Show me the way to the House of Handbags!" cried Sophia, finishing her honeycomb ice cream in one big gulp. "We need all the information we can get!"

Kit, Caleb, Sophia and Rufus set off at a march across the square following Joni's directions. But Joni was adamant she wasn't going back to the mysteriously magical handbag shop. She couldn't risk falling under its spell again and buying up half the handbags!

Elodie, Marnie-Mae and Joni looked around for somewhere to hide out so Skylar could relax. She was still very alarmed, her panic making Elodie's hair fizz and crackle. But every inch of every elegant paving stone was crowded with keen-eyed tourists posing for pictures, trying on Venetian masks or devouring great slabs of pizza.

Elodie softly pressed her forehead to the unicorn's

downy brow and at once she felt the pull of the sea: it was singing to her.

"I think Skylar wants to be the near the water," she said.

"Makes sense," agreed Marnie. "She is a Surf Dancer."

Skylar turned towards a glittering stretch of sea where a group of smiling holidaymakers were forming a queue by a little wooden pier.

"That's the perfect solution!" said Joni, following Skylar's gaze "Let's take a ride on a gondola!"

The two friends grinned with glee, happily joining the queue. Skylar stepped confidently into the little boat, making all the Venetians coo with affection. With her sunglasses still in place and her horn gently shimmering, she squeezed between Elodie and Marnie. Joni also seemed to be in her element, her sun hat tilted back and her sandals kicked off as she enjoyed the sights.

The gondolier steered them through a maze of little waterways lined with beautiful historic homes, whose balconies above the ancient doorways were bursting with flowers. They passed a wildly romantic theatre spilling notes of opera through its open door, and wonderful churches whose towering spires reached towards the sky. It felt like they were drifting through a different time, where art and culture and wonderment ruled.

Slowly the lull of the water soothed the unicorn's heart back to contentment, and beside her Elodie and Marnie-Mae relaxed, giggling as Skylar's sea-foam mane danced on the breeze and Marnie's braids flowed out behind her quite beautifully.

At the entrance to the House of Handbags, just outside the golden-rose archway, Caleb paused. The shop itself was both chic and simple. There was a spaciousness to it, a sense of freedom in the high ceilings and tall windows, and, even though Caleb had never owned nor wanted a handbag in his life, he found himself drawn to the inviting scent of leather and lavender.

But Rufus gave a low growl and Caleb turned his attention away from the shop and sat down on its large doorstep with his faithful friend beside him.

"Good idea. You wait here with Rufus," said

Sophia reassuringly, sensing Caleb's unease.

Kit and Sophia stepped into the luxurious shop, instantly dazzled by an array of stunning bags in vivid and glorious colours.

"It's like being inside a rainbow," murmured Kit, peering around in quiet amazement. Everywhere he looked something spectacular caught his eye.

He blinked at the notebook in his hands, reminding himself to stay focused.

"Ciao, can I help you?" asked a glamorous woman dripping with diamonds and flowing silk scarves.

"Yes," said Kit brightly, noticing his mum had already fallen under the shop's dark spell and was clutching an enormous scarlet shoulder bag, large enough to hold a yoga mat.

"I'm here on a history trip and I'd love to do some research on your shop!" he said brightly, trying not get distracted by a lovely purple leather wallet.

"Certainly." The woman smiled at him while deftly directing Sophia towards the till. Luckily, she was at the back of a queue of very excitable Americans who appeared to be buying up half the shop, so Kit knew he had a bit of time before he needed to rescue her.

"What exactly would you like to know?"

"When was the shop established?" Kit asked confidently.

The woman simpered. "Over a hundred years ago," she said. "Before my grandfather was even born. He is our oldest family member. He remembers when the business was just a stall on the beach. And, thanks to him, it has grown into the most famous handbag emporium in Venice."

"And where are the handbags actually made?" Kit continued, trying to keep an eye on Sophia.

"In our warehouse near my grandfather's home on the Lido di Venezia."

"That's actually where we're headed next," said Kit, improvising. "I don't suppose you do tours?"

"Sadly not," the woman answered, seeming a little bored with their conversation by now.

"What's the proprietor, your grandfather, called?"

"Alberto Stregone," she answered.

"So what's his secret?" Kit asked and the woman narrowed her eyes at him.

"To running such a famous shop?" Kit said with a gulp and she recovered her smile. "Talent, work, family and love." She beamed, moving away from Kit to help a group of German backpackers who seemed very surprised to find themselves in the House of Handbags.

"Time to go, Mum," said Kit, quickly pulling Sophia away from the queue and towards the door.

The moment she put the scarlet shoulder bag down, the group of Americans at the till all shook their heads in confusion, and decided to purchase one gorgeous suede suitcase instead of ten. The Germans backpackers snapped out of their trance and hurriedly followed Kit and Sophia out of the shop along with half the other customers.

All of them, Kit noticed, were empty-handed.

"The magic is fading," he murmured, scribbling it down quickly in his notebook as they reached the grand doorstep.

Caleb and Rufus were sitting in the sunshine beside a little girl with long brown hair and large curious eyes.

"And that's where the unicorn lives. No one ever believes me, but it's completely true," she was saying, chattering away quite contentedly.

"I believe you," Caleb mumbled, stroking Rufus.

Kit and Sophia kept very still, not wanting to interrupt the conversation.

"She only comes out at night, and her favourite food is pistachio gelato and salty chips."

Caleb shrugged. "All the unicorns I know like

gluten-free muffins."

"Gluten-free! Yuck!" cried the child, looking appalled.

"Francesca! Back inside, please. It's almost time for your dance class!" called the glamorous woman, leaning out of the shop. Francesca leapt to her feet and skipped through the golden-rose archway.

"We've got the name of proprietor," Kit whispered, kneeling beside his brother.

"And the secret location," Caleb said, giving a big, dreamy yawn. He was feeling rather sleepy, despite it still being the morning. He was ready for a nap before the real adventure began.

CHAPTER TEN
MOONLIGHT IN VENICE

As the moon rose over Venice, like a huge gleaming pearl reflected on the sea, the Unicorn Seekers of South London were ready. They had spent all afternoon perfecting their outfits – and finally it was time to set off.

Joni had had the wild idea to go in disguise when they visited the handbag warehouse. She was loving the element of mystery that swirled through the streets of Venice in the form of theatrical masks.

Marnie-Mae had bound her braids up into a spectacular bun on top of her head. Her face was half covered by a striking purple mask in the shape of a butterfly that was very beautiful.

Beside her, Kit wore a mask of vivid emerald

green, edged in feathers like the wings of a parakeet. It reminded him of home yet whispered of freedom and high open skies.

Caleb had chosen a mask that was winter-themed, as that was his favourite season. It sparkled with breathtaking snowflakes of turquoise and white, making him look like a modern-day Jack Frost.

Elodie had decided on a silver mask of magnificent craftsmanship. It was shaped like the moon and stars and studded with jewels the colour of midnight. It matched her hair when it crackled with blue lightning.

Sophia's mask was a delicate lilac and sculped like a lotus. It sat perfectly on her nose, covering her eyes and forehead.

Joni herself had gone for a simple but stunning mask of glittering gold with ruby-red lips and dark-lined eyes, which covered all her face.

And at the centre of the little huddle of friends, trotting with her head held high, came Skylar, wearing a sea-themed mask depicting a wave. It made her look very regal.

Any late-night revellers who passed this strange group would assume they were part of an impressive circus troupe.

"Where do we get the ferry from?" asked Elodie, who was at the front of the group with Caleb, both their hands resting tenderly upon Skylar's neck.

"Right there," Kit answered, gesturing to one of the many jetties where tourists were gathered. And sure enough, in among the water taxis and small boats, came a ferry with a large open deck, called a vaporetto, which was headed for Lido di Venezia – the Lido island.

The ferry crew were not at all worried about Skylar boarding the boat. As long as she had a ticket, she was deemed a worthy customer and they were very happy to welcome her.

"That was easy." Marnie grinned, half her smile hidden by the butterfly mask.

"Maybe they know Skylar?" Caleb whispered. "They seem very familiar with her."

The crew were indeed very friendly to Skylar. They spent the journey singing and dancing and trying to pat her ears, much to Elodie's alarm. Elodie had bound her dancing curls up into a ponytail, but they still fizzed and zapped with lightning any time anyone got too close to Skylar.

The ferry sailed past many wondrous landmarks and then made for the open sea, following a trail of shimmering sea-lamps all the way to the Lido island.

As they clambered off the boat, waving farewell to the crew of singing sailors, they found themselves on one of the most charming islands imaginable.

Elodie smiled, her shoulders relaxing as she took in the call of night birds and the floating laughter that echoed around them.

The atmosphere was different here, a place of sea-swept beauty and summer warmth. All the restaurants were still open and in no rush to close. It was like stepping into the heart of a holiday.

Skylar gave a soft shake of her mane and trotted swiftly along the main street. Her nose twitched as she followed the scent of the sea.

"Maybe this is where she's from. She seems to know it really well," said Sophia as they hurried to keep up.

"I wish we'd brought our skates," Kit grumbled.

"I don't – I can hardly see anything in this mask!" cried Marnie-Mae, accidentally stumbling into him.

Skylar led them down a long road full of dazzling hotels and blossoming gardens. The opposite side of the road was broken up by a series of wooden gates leading to boathouses, sailing clubs or beachside cafes, before giving way to the glorious starlit sea.

"Private beaches where the waiters bring you champagne!" breathed Joni, peeking out from behind her golden ruby mask. "This is my kind of island."

"Do you think the House of Handbags warehouse is near here?" asked Sophia, whose vision was partly obscured by her lilac lotus mask so she was relying on Rufus to guide her.

Caleb stood still, frowning as he studied the rough sketch he'd drawn from Francesca's description. He gave a shrug, not really sure where they were.

Elodie peered at the beach beyond the boathouses.

It was lovely, but it was nothing like the one in her dream. She closed her eyes behind her moon-and-stars mask, feeling through the salty night air for Skylar's thoughts. But all she could sense was the steady rhythm of the unicorn's heart, beating in time with the pounding of her hooves.

"No," she said slowly. "I think it's somewhere else."

Together the masked group moved deeper into the island down a smaller road lined with swaying trees and streetlamps. When they came to a little refreshment van, Kit bought a portion of chips. It was just what the adventure needed, he felt.

Skylar eventually paused at a stretch of empty beach, her head flicking from left to right, her mane catching in the night breeze.

The others looked around. Beautiful white driftwood benches were dotted along the stone pier and a strange ominous-looking shed loomed near the water's edge.

Elodie took off her mask and gazed about. It was hard to tell if this was the beach from her dream, but there was a strange magic to its sparseness. She could feel it and her hair was quietly zapping and zinging. Beside her, Caleb stopped at the edge of the sand and studied the landscape. He was quite enjoying wearing his snowflake mask and thought perhaps he might wear it every day from now on.

"This isn't the beach from my dream, but it matches Francesca's description," he said, pointing at his sketch.

"So what do we do – just wait?" asked Marnie-Mae.

As they stared at the forbidding shape of the warehouse, they saw faint lights flickering within. Caleb instinctively hid between Skylar and Rufus, the soft feel of Skylar's mane reassuring him.

"We should stay hidden," said Sophia.

"No," said Joni brightly. "I've got a better idea. Whoever's inside that warehouse has to come out on to the beach so we can get inside to find this Delphi – right?"

"Yes," came a murmur of voices soft as the wind.

"But we need to protect Skylar as well. We don't want the House of Handbags taking her instead," said Elodie quickly.

"I'll stay with Skylar," volunteered Caleb, trying

to coax the wild-hearted unicorn gently into the shadows. But Skylar was reluctant to move, her grey eyes flashing.

"Try these." Kit passed his tray of chips to his brother.

Caleb gingerly held out a handful of slightly cold seaside chips to the majestic creature before him and was quite amazed when she snaffled them up. With a grateful grin, he stepped backwards into the safety of some shadowy trees. And Skylar followed.

"Well, that's something I didn't know!" chuckled Marnie. "Surf Dancers like really salty chips."

"Makes sense, I guess" said Elodie quietly. "You can always get them at the seaside."

"Here," said Kit going over to his brother and giving him some of their carefully saved holiday money. "Buy some more snacks and see what else Skylar likes."

A cool breeze blew in making everyone shiver.

"Right, let's give the staff of the House of Handbags a reason to come out on to the beach at this time of night! We'll distract them with a show!" cried Joni, kicking off her sandals ready to dance.

Five minutes later, a performance of splendour and moonlight and chaos began to unfold. It started with the beat of a driftwood drum – which Kit had found behind a rock. Then Marnie-Mae and Elodie tore across the beach in a whirl of synchronized cartwheels, whipping up the sand in a silvery spray.

Behind them, Joni started dancing with such joy and energy, it was as if she was at a carnival in Jamaica. Sophia trailed peacefully at the back, chanting soulfully and performing moon yoga as Rufus ran in great circles round the merry little procession.

A bright beam of light fell across the sand and a muffled, giddy yell reached their ears. They froze mid-step, staring at a little girl with long brown hair and curious eyes who was sitting on a unicorn cut from the beauty of the sea and the grace of the moon.

From the Speranza memoir: *In Hope of Magic*

Chapter Seven

The Ball of Floating Stars

Tonight is the night. I am waiting for my sweet Graciella under the winged statue that faces the sea. The stars are reflecting so beautifully upon the water, it seems that you could swim through the night sky.

I see now how the ball got its name. It's beautiful, even if it is hosted by the Stregone family, who I know are killing unicorns. And the worst thing about it is they have no remorse: they believe they're doing nothing wrong. They tame the unicorns, keep them close, win their trust, like a wild horse you might keep on the beach or at the bottom of your garden. But then every fifty years or so they sacrifice one... All in the name of fashion.

The music is starting! I can hear the flutes and lutes and perhaps even a harp. And the masks and gowns really are quite wonderful.

My heart is beating so fast. I see young Alberto through the great doors with the unicorn beside him; they seem so fond of each other. The sight pains my heart. But my bold Graciella is with me. She looks marvellous in a mask the shape of a dark-winged moth.

I am never afraid when I'm with Graciella. Her courage shall spur me on. We will enter the ball together and, with luck, it will not simply be a ball but a rescue mission.

I will report on our progress tomorrow,
Giovanni

CHAPTER ELEVEN

A THREAD OF GLITTERING SEA-LIGHT

The unicorn was like Skylar, but sleeker, wilder and completely iridescent. Every inch of her sparkled like a dream of celestial grace.

None of the Unicorn Seekers had ever seen anyone ride a unicorn before. Nor had they imagined it possible. It would be like trying to ride a deer, or a fox, or a fierce wolf in the wild. Unicorns were feral and wild and not meant to be tamed.

Elodie studied the little girl and the astonishing creature. Squeezing her eyes shut behind her starry mask, ignoring the zing of her electric curls, she reached out with her mind, trying to sense the unicorn. At first, there was only the crash of the waves and rush of the sea, but then flickering at the edge of her thoughts, like a light in the dark, she felt the creature.

And what she sensed surprised her greatly. It was nothing but loyalty and love.

This spellbinding Surf Dancer, Delphi, was bonded to the little girl, Francesca, in a way Elodie had never known. It brought tears to her eyes, reminding her of the special bond she'd had with Astra, the first unicorn she'd ever seen, and then with little Stormy, the baby unicorn they'd rescued in the autumn.

The bond between Francesca and Delphi was like a thread of glittering sea-light, the colour of pearls and mist, but strong as diamonds. Elodie knew then, with a terrible jolt, that they could not be separated. Francesca must be a deeply gifted seeker, like Elodie's great-grandmother, Elyse de Lyon, had been.

This child loved the unicorn. And the unicorn loved the child so fiercely she would protect her always.

Delphi would give her life for Francesca, Elodie realized with a gasp.

"Would you like to join in our show?" called Kit, banging his driftwood drum. "All people and horses are welcome," he continued, trying not to make it obvious that the Unicorn Seekers could see the unicorn, her dazzling shimmer and the glints of her horn catching in the starlight.

"I'd love to!" cried Francesca, and at once Delphi galloped towards them, covering the beach in seashell hoofprints.

Behind her, a figure appeared in the doorway of the warehouse, and Elodie's blood ran cold. This was the splendidly dressed old gentleman from her dream. She could tell from the unmistakable cut of his hat, and the polished leather brogues he wore – even on the beach!

As he strode towards them, it was easy to see that though he was elderly, maybe even a hundred years old, he was still agile and dynamic.

"Francesca!" he cried, the air filling with a stream of Italian sentences that were spoken with such flourish and expression it was like listening to a song.

Delphi paused as the old man spoke, her eyes

radiant, but Elodie could feel a flicker of defiance. As if the unicorn understood him perfectly, yet didn't want to obey.

Maybe Delphi knows he's dangerous, thought Elodie, her hair crackling so much it made her dizzy.

Francesca answered the man just as vividly in Italian and he went back into the warehouse. She turned to face the masked troupe before her.

"I have to go back inside in a few minutes," she explained. "I've got to practise my dance for the legendary ball my great-grandfather throws every year."

"Is that your great-granddad?" asked Kit, thinking back to the conversation he'd had with Francesca's mother, and the name of the proprietor he'd scribbled in his notebook.

Alberto Stregone.

"Yes." Francesca nodded.

"What ball?" piped up Marnie, hoping that her purple butterfly mask would fully disguise her, and the little girl wouldn't recognize her or any of the others from earlier that morning.

"The Ball of Floating Stars," breathed Francesca

excitedly, her eyes gleaming almost as brightly as her unicorn's.

In the sea-scented dark, Marnie-Mae reached for Elodie's hand and squeezed it hard.

Elodie leaned in close as Marnie whispered to her, "Elle – that's the name of the ball in your great-grandmother's letter!"

Elodie nodded in understanding, and then the driftwood drum began to beat again, and Sophia sang while Joni danced. Elodie and Marnie-Mae started to turn cartwheels again, laughing and kicking up the sand.

Francesca clapped and whooped, then she surprised everyone by leaping from the unicorn's back and dancing, stamping and singing as loud as she could. Even Delphi pawed the sand with her hoof in time to the music. The waves crashed and the surf lapped round their ankles, making everyone squeal.

Then, quite suddenly, Delphi turned her head and began to gallop up the beach faster than flight – straight towards the leafy shadows where Skylar and Caleb were hiding.

Francesca called out in Italian, her brow furrowed,

wondering what her precious unicorn was up to.

"So tell us more about the ball," said Elodie loudly, trying to draw the little girl's attention away from the beating heart of Skylar.

"It's the grandest masquerade ball in Venice," was all Francesca said, her thoughts clearly distracted, perhaps sensing the presence of another unicorn shimmering softly at the edge of her mind.

"How do we get tickets?" asked Marnie-Mae.

Francesca shrugged. "You can't – it's by invitation only. And only the oldest families in Venice, who've known my great-grandpa since for ever, are allowed to attend.

"We may not be from an old Italian family," said Joni smoothly, her golden mask glinting sharply in the moonlight, "but we are a famed theatre troupe who perform all over the world. Perhaps I could speak to your great-grandfather and see if he'll make an exception?"

Everyone held their breath, but Francesca just laughed at this notion.

"My great-grandpa makes the rules, and he never changes them for anyone," she said with another shrug before setting off up the beach after Delphi.

Through the eyeholes of many theatrical masks, the Unicorn Seekers peered at each other anxiously, uncertain what to do. They were relieved that Alberto had vanished back into the warehouse earlier, thankfully unaware of a second unicorn so close by.

Quickly, Elodie and Marnie turned to follow Francesca. She was very fast and nimble on her feet, barely stirring the sand as she darted over it.

"We have to stop her before she finds Skylar," Elodie hissed.

Just as Francesca reached the little pathway that led to the leafy shadows, Caleb appeared in his snowflake mask with Delphi trotting calmly beside him, his hand resting gently on her nose as she fondly nuzzled his hair.

Francesca stopped short, peering at Caleb in amazement before muttering, "Thank you." She clearly wasn't used to other people bonding with her unicorn.

"Francesca!" came her great-grandfather's voice from across the sand and she reluctantly said goodbye, swinging herself effortlessly up on to Delphi's back.

Caleb marvelled at how at ease the unicorn and the little girl were with each other, but he was careful not to speak, in case Francesca remembered him from before.

The little troupe waved farewell, staring in quiet awe as Delphi galloped smoothly away across the night sand and into the warehouse.

Once the doors had swung closed, and they could hear the soft swell of violin music swirling through the air, everyone flocked round Caleb.

"That was amazing," said Sophia proudly. "Well done for protecting Skylar."

Caleb didn't say anything, but he gave a small smile.

"I found loads of other foods that Skylar likes," he murmured. "Gelato – especially mint-choc-chip – churros and cherry syrup!"

Everyone laughed at this.

"Where's Skylar now?" asked Elodie, glancing around.

"Right here," Caleb mumbled, patting a patch of air beside him, which slowly shimmered and then seemed to part as Skylar stepped daintily on to the beach, as if she was emerging from a dream.

Elodie sighed. "She can't stay with us any longer," she said sorrowfully. "It just isn't safe for her here. We can't risk the House of Handbags discovering her."

"Are you sure we can't just keep her hidden at our hotel?" pleaded Marnie-Mae. "I could stay with her – you know, get room service and stuff."

The others all smiled ruefully, knowing it was impossible.

Elodie stepped forward and closed her eyes, resting her forehead against the beautiful Surf Dancer's brow. Beaming nothing but love, she sent her thoughts to the graceful creature as she gently removed her mask.

You must go. It's not safe here.

Skylar kept very still until Elodie moved back. She blinked her sea-grey eyes and her horn flashed dangerously in the moonlight. She turned to each of the Unicorn Seekers, meeting their gaze with a burning intelligence or nuzzling their cheeks. When she came to Caleb, she bowed regally, her horn touching his shoulders, like a queen and a knight.

And then she reared up powerfully on the beach

and raced towards the sea, vanishing in a cloud of sand and starlight before she reached the waves.

"It's all right," said Joni, who was weeping behind her golden mask, as she gathered everyone into a big group hug. Even poor Rufus, who was howling sorrowfully.

"She's a creature of sea and surf. She'll find somewhere safe."

They all huddled together in the salty dark before setting off back to the ferry port.

Nobody felt like talking, but they all held hands as they wandered the warm, gelato-scented streets.

Sophia's phone pinged and she gave a little gasp. "It's another message from Anisha and Rishi." She smiled. "Rishi's found something in the Library of South London that might just help us."

They stopped at a cafe in the harbour, which was selling late-night drinks and sorbet, to read the extract from the Speranzas' memoir.

"So," said Kit, scribbling furiously in his notebook, "we just need to find this Speranza family. They're our ticket to the Ball of Floating Stars."

Everyone ate their sorbet in silence. Tomorrow

was going to be a big day. They had a ball to attend and a unicorn to rescue.

It was only Caleb who felt a soft nuzzling on his shoulder and, turning his head, noticed that all the ice-cream-cone crumbs were rapidly disappearing, as if an invisible little animal was gobbling them up. When they set off again towards the ferry port, he was heartened to spot a pale unicorn-shaped shadow trailing them.

He smiled into the starry dark and kept Skylar's secret.

CHAPTER TWELVE

THE FORGOTTEN INVITATION

The next morning, they awoke to the cries of seabirds and tour guides echoing through the winding streets and waterways of Venice.

Kit was up first, busily researching the Speranzas as he munched on a breakfast of chocolate cornetti and freshly squeezed lemon juice. It was rather sharp but very refreshing.

It had been easy to find plenty of information online, and it was helping him keep his mind off the sadness of saying goodbye to yet another beautiful unicorn.

As he read from his iPad, he learned that the Speranzas had once been a formidable family with a shoe empire, who worked in collaboration with the Stregone family – until they fell out and became competitors instead.

"Can I get you anything else, young sir?" asked a friendly member of the hotel staff, whose name badge said Stephano.

"No, *grazie*," Kit replied, hoping he'd said 'thank you' correctly in Italian. The man smiled at him kindly.

"Are you learning Italian?" asked Stephano, gesturing to Kit's notes.

"No, I'm researching a feud between two of the leading families in Venice," Kit explained excitedly.

Stephano raised an eyebrow in interest.

"The Speranza and the Stregone families," Kit went on.

"What do you wish to know?" asked Stephano with a wide grin.

"Why they fell out?" Kit asked eagerly.

"It's a fascinating tale!" the young man cried, putting down his coffee pot and leaning forward eagerly. "I can tell you all the details! My cousin's next-door neighbour, Loreta, is a Speranza. Her very own grandparents, Graciella and Giovanni, were at the ball that fateful night."

Kit's eyes widened as Stephano began his extraordinary tale.

"It all began on the night of the Ball of Floating Stars seventy-five years ago... The story goes that Graciella and Giovanni were there on a very important mission. You see, Graciella was determined to set free the Stregone family's cherished horse. It had some kind of majestic pedigree and the Stregones were planning to sacrifice it and use the leather for their exquisite handbags. Graciella was very, very against that."

Kit nodded, knowing that Graciella and Giovanni had been trying to save a unicorn.

"Graciella entered the ballroom wearing the mask of a dark-winged moth. Giovanni was dressed in a cape of sweeping black and his mask was that of an owl.

"There was a grand spectacle in the centre of the ball, set to the tune of a thousand violins, where the youngest member of the Stregone family, Alberto, and the pedigree horse performed together. While Giovanni kept watch, Graciella climbed up to the ornate ceiling of the ballroom and then descended on a wire, into the centre of the dance, like a great falling moth. She knocked Alberto to the ground and set the beautiful horse free.

"But it was utter chaos! The horse – who was dressed as a unicorn, charged wildly into the crowd, injuring people as it went, its prop horn ruining ballgowns, spilling wine, damaging masks. Tears fell freely. People fainted from shock. Alberto ran to find his beloved pet, but his family got there first, capturing the horse with a lasso that crackled as blue as lightning. The poor beast was fatally injured.

Young Alberto never forgave Graciella or Giovanni, and his family banned them from ever attending another ball."

"So the poor uni— I mean horse died anyway?" mumbled Kit, feeling a little queasy.

"I am afraid so."

"And what of the Speranzas?"

"Graciella and Giovanni married and moved their family's shoe company to Florence. I believe most of them are still there."

"And do you know if Loreta, or any other member of the Speranza family, or even you have ever been back to the Ball of Floating Stars?" asked Kit, his heart hammering with hope.

Stephano frowned and shook his head. "I would love to go, but I'm no relation, and besides, as I mentioned, the last time the Speranzas were invited was seventy-five years ago."

"How do you know all this?" asked Kit, quite amazed.

Stefano grinned. "I'm very interested in history: it's the reason I came to Venice. My cousin works at the Leonardo da Vinci Museum, and he's an expert at tracking down precious things. He's got half the Speranza family artefacts in his attic, including Graciella's wedding dress, the dark moth mask and the tear-stained invitation. He keeps a lot of heirlooms safe for Loretta, with the hope that one day they'll have gathered enough artefacts for a little exhibition."

Kit nearly leapt out of his chair in eagerness. "Who's to say that invitation can't be used again?" he said as Joni wandered into the breakfast room, huge black sunglasses firmly in place, despite the lack of sunshine in the quaint little room.

She smiled and introduced herself to Stephano as she sought out a decaf mocha.

"What if my friends and I borrowed the invitation and said we were the young Speranzas coming in peace, wanting to put an end to the feud between our families?" asked Kit.

Stephano chuckled, but then his expression grew serious. "An impossible request," he said with a sigh. "And the wrong time for such a proposal. The Stregone empire is struggling; it is rumoured their sales are way down and that they're very close to going bankrupt!"

Joni took a long sip of her steaming decaf before speaking. "What if we approached them and offered to do a mega social-media post about how we'd all love to work together on a shoe and handbag collaboration like hashtag-putting-the-past-to-rest? Or hashtag-investing-in-future-generations?"

Stephano considered this carefully. "The Venetia House of Handbags has been losing business for a long time now. They definitely need a new direction…"

"Really?" piped up Marnie-Mae as she sat down at the next table with Elodie, to a breakfast of fresh fruit and buttery soft croissants – full of gluten!

Stephano nodded. "Yes. Whatever power and influence they once had seems to be fading."

"That's why they need Delphi," Elodie murmured darkly to Marnie.

"Do you think we could ask your cousin and Loreta if we could borrow the tear-stained invitation and try to get into the ball?" Kit asked.

Stephano had said that Loreta was Graciella and

Giovanni's granddaughter. If the Speranza family memoir was anything to go by, they'd both been Unicorn Seekers, so there was a strong possibility that Loreta was one too.

Kit took a deep breath, for luck – the way he did just before he perfected a skate trick and said, "Please tell Loreta it's for a unicorn."

Stephano gave him an odd look, but agreed, sauntering away to make a phone call.

Sophia came in and began gathering a plate of food for Caleb. He was staying cosily in bed with Rufus, but was eager to try out a variety of different foods much to Sophia's delight.

Stephano came hurrying back into the breakfast room. "I spoke with my cousin and to Loreta! Normally, she would say a firm no to such a plan," he explained, looking pleasantly surprised, "but when I mentioned the unicorn, she knew at once you must have read the Speranza memoir! It's been such a long time since she's come across an avid historian she was quite charmed. She gives her full permission for you to use the invitation, as long as I attend with you and she herself accompanies us!"

All the Unicorn Seekers were speechless, staring open-mouthed in amazement.

"So we're actually going to the legendary Ball of Floating Stars with a member of the famous Speranza family?" chirruped Marnie.

"Of course we are!" beamed Joni, opening her fan.

"If they let us in," said Stephano with a sigh. "Right, I'll meet you all by the basilica in St Mark's Square at seven p.m. In the meantime, find some fancy clothes! This year's theme is summer flowers."

And, just like that, the Unicorn Seekers of South London had an (almost) invitation to the most prestigious ball of their young lives. And a real chance to save Delphi.

Letter from Graciella to Giovanni

My dearest Gio,

I hope this letter finds you well. I write from the safety of Florence, where I fled after the Ball of Floating Stars, and am in hiding but quite comfortable. I have the use of a huge empty attic, where I am alone with the birds and can see over the entire city.

It is quite beautiful. Perhaps we should all move here and continue your family's shoe empire far from Venice.

I am still heartbroken over that poor unicorn, Leonardo. He was so magnificent, and now he is lost. I know we did our very best to free him. It was a cruel and clever trick the Stregones used, making it look like it was our fault. That he ran wild because of us and they had no choice but to end his life, to protect the people at the ball.

And what of poor little Alberto? Will he ever learn the terrible truth? And how will his young heart not break into a thousand pieces? I don't know the answers, nor how we will continue to protect the Surf Dancers we are called to serve, but I shall devote my life to it.

There will be many more unicorns to save — just think of all those we have already freed! We must not let this one terrible occurrence stop us. There are so many of these beautiful creatures who need our help.

In fact, just yesterday I spied another in a Florentine market. Not a Surf Dancer, but a creature of exquisite beauty, nonetheless. I believe her to be a Twilight Grace — a Mist and Rain unicorn.

I will endeavour to help her find her glory. And, in the meantime, perhaps you can try to make contact with young Alberto?

And yes, I do accept your proposal of marriage! As soon as circumstances are calmer, we shall be wed beneath the stars.

Yours truly for ever and ever,
Graciella

CHAPTER THIRTEEN

THE BALL OF FLOATING STARS

The evening sun hovered in the sky, slowly turning from warm gold to sunset pink, and in the hotel room the four friends all stared at each other in delight. They were almost unrecognizable in their flower-themed outfits and matching masks.

After a wild morning of shopping, Joni and Sophia had spent the afternoon stitching and fixing and adjusting the outfits so they were worthy of appearing at a fairy-tale ball.

Elodie was a sunflower, her beautiful curls brushed out in a halo round her mask. Her dress was sewn from different yellow beach towels in a wonderful patchwork that reached her ankles.

Kit was a poppy, his suit a vibrant red, his mask

made of three separate pieces that cleverly overlapped. He had even painted his entire chin red with Joni's lipstick. It was a very dramatic look.

Marnie-Mae was a pale pink peony, her outfit made from overlapping tutus, a pink swimsuit and a big pink ruff around her neck. Her mask was shimmery and quite mesmerizing.

And Caleb, who didn't want to give up his winter-themed mask, had gone as a snow-flower. Dressed in a spectacular cloak made from bedsheets, his arms and hands were painted white with sun cream.

"We look awesome! We should definitely put a pic on the blog," said Marnie, snapping away on her mum's phone.

"Are you ready?" asked Sophia, gazing at them proudly. They nodded, all keenly aware of the plan.

The Unicorn Seekers, along with Loreta and Stephano, would attempt to enter the ball while Joni and Sophia created a distraction, hopefully making it easier for the others to get in.

They gathered together for a great big group hug, squeezing poor Rufus in the middle. Caleb was a little nervous about leaving Rufus with the mums, but he knew if it meant saving a unicorn then he would do it.

Out into the summer streets of Venice they walked, delighting in the smiles and compliments they got from passers-by.

Stephano looked quite astonished when he saw them approaching. "Well, it's certainly a modern take on fancy evening wear," he said, gazing in awe at the sun cream, lipstick, bedsheets, beach towels and tutus.

"Exactly," beamed Joni, who had transformed her sarong into a quite dazzling toga. She looked like a Greek goddess in sunglasses. Beside her lingered Sophia in a far more low-key mauve outfit, which matched her lotus mask.

"They'll be a social-media sensation," she said with a wink and Stephano clapped his hands in appreciation.

"Allow me to introduce you to Loreta Speranza," he said in a low, mysterious voice. Stepping aside, he revealed a glamorous woman draped in a gown of emerald velvet with a marvellous matching leaf mask and a big velvet hat.

She glowed with happiness at the sight of the Unicorn Seekers. Opening her arms to them in appreciation, she began singing their praises in Italian.

And then it was time to say a quick goodbye to Rufus, Joni and Sophia and follow Stephano to a ballroom at the edge of the sea where early starlight was softly flickering on the water.

"Invitations, please?" The security guards smiled, clearly charmed by the Unicorn Seekers' costumes.

Loreta swiftly produced the invitation from many years ago, the tear stains carefully removed, the date slightly obscured.

"Speranza?" queried a burly security guard with a fantastic moustache that Kit was very impressed by.

"Yes," piped up Marnie-Mae. "We're the new generation of hope."

"From London, but with our hearts in Italy," added Kit quickly.

Elodie stepped forward, her hair crackling magnetically, almost hypnotizing the guards, and began the little speech she'd rehearsed with Sophia.

"We have an appointment with Alberto himself to discuss a new direction for the brand—"

The frowning guard held up a hand to stop her, looking rather bored. Elodie, slightly taken aback, held her head higher, thinking only of the beautiful unicorn inside whose fierce energy she could feel pulling at her heart.

"It's all true," said Stephano in Italian, but the guards ignored him.

Loreta eyed the men coolly and was about to launch into a spectacular rant when there came a dramatic cry from behind her.

"Out of my way! I demand to be let in!" said a loud, confident voice as Joni tried to barge past the Unicorn Seekers. Sophia was hovering around her like the perfect assistant, carrying her hat and bag. They had the same masks on as before; Sophia's lotus mask was perfect for the theme of the ball. And, even though Joni wasn't technically a flower, she looked like a radiant moonflower in the gold and ruby mask.

"Invitation!" barked another of the guards.

"Don't you know who I am?" exclaimed Joni, pretending to take great offence and batting the guard with her fan, while Sophia began calmly but loudly chanting in the guard's face.

"We don't want to keep Alberto waiting," said Stephano anxiously as he pretended to check his watch. The big guard with the fabulous moustache glanced around uncertainly.

"I'd hate to disappoint Francesca. She's expecting me to help her with the show," said Caleb suddenly, sounding very worried indeed. At the mention of Francesca, the guard softened and quickly ushered them all through, while more guards arrived to deal with the small crowd of onlookers that had gathered round Joni and Sophia, and who were clearly enjoying the spectacle.

As the others stepped into a ballroom of dazzling elegance, they fell under the spell of its splendour. Then Elodie shook her head, her curls crackling with wild blue light.

"Everything is sprinkled with unicorn dust," she breathed, feeling horrified.

"What do you mean, unicorn dust?" asked Stephano with a warm chuckle. "Don't tell me you believe the Speranza family memoir?"

"We just want to find out if there's any truth in them." Kit smiled through his poppy-petal mask.

And, to his delight, Loreta smiled back at him from behind her emerald-green leaf mask.

Suddenly the orchestra began to play. The lights dimmed low, so the only illumination came from the candlelit chandeliers, and everyone swirled on to the dance floor. Caleb hid behind a large pillar, refusing to dance, and Elodie stayed with him so she could keep an eye out for Francesca, but Kit, Marnie-Mae and even Stephano found themselves pulled helplessly into the crowd of swirling dancers. Swept up in a whirl of velvet and sequins, they joined the mysterious masked dancers.

"At least I can see in this mask," joked Marnie, clinging on to Kit so they didn't get separated.

Kit laughed. "This would be more fun on skates," he said, trying not to tread on the toes of an elegant woman in a gold dress. He stumbled and almost fell when he realized it was Francesca's mother.

Elodie peered round the room, trying not to laugh at her friend's terrible attempts to dance.

"They're so bad," muttered Caleb, who could hardly bring himself to watch.

"But Stephano is very good," Elodie whispered as they watched him glide smoothly round the room with Loreta.

Beyond the great window, the sun faded to twilight and then night fell. As the dancing continued, an array of mouth-watering delicacies arrived, served on silver platters. Blackcurrant tartlets, candied lemons, chocolate-filled gnocchi, as well as apricot cordial and champagne for the grown-ups.

Elodie and Caleb sampled everything, then began to feel a little sick from all the sugary foods.

"Do you think we should go and find Francesca?" Elodie murmured to Caleb, but all at once the room fell into a whispering hush, the dancing stilled and all eyes turned to the middle of the room. There was little Francesca, bright-eyed as ever, dressed as a magnolia flower, sitting on the back of her gleaming unicorn.

The crowd gasped and swooned, quite astounded.

Clearly, they thought this was all part of a marvellous act.

Elodie's hair flashed a vivid blue: she could sense Delphi's unease at the situation. She blinked and rubbed her eyes through her sunflower mask.

"Can everyone here see Delphi as a unicorn?" she asked Caleb.

"Yes." He nodded. "It must be the dust – it's given everyone Unicorn Sight, but they think they're seeing special effects."

They all watched with their hearts in their throats as Francesca and Delphi performed a slow-moving waltz. Francesca pirouetted gracefully on Delphi's back while Delphi trotted and pranced with a ballerina's lightness.

But the unicorn's thoughts were whirring with a bright, jagged energy that both Caleb and Elodie found overwhelming.

Alberto strode on to the dance floor, bowing regally to his many admirers, who in their costumes looked like a sea of adoring flowers.

He made a lengthy speech in Italian, which none of the Unicorn Seekers could understand. Stephano

was on the other side of the room talking very passionately with a fine young gentleman in the corner, so there was no way he could translate for them.

Kit and Marnie-Mae watched through the crowd, Kit desperately trying to translate everything on his mum's phone. Elodie and Caleb peered out from behind a pillar as a beautiful ornate wagon was wheeled into the centre of the dance floor and a new act began.

First, there was a quiver on the cello, then a flutter on the flute, a harmony on the harp, and finally a thousand violins filled the air.

"This is very bad," gasped Caleb. "This is Delphi's final act."

Elodie clutched her heart in horror as the performance started.

A woman moved into the spotlight, holding an ornate birdcage that had a nightingale inside. She opened the bars and the little thing flew straight into the wagon. The doors were closed and then opened on both sides, the wagon slowly turning so everyone could see that the little bird had vanished, and the wagon was completely empty.

The crowd *oohed* and *aahed*.

Next a young boy stepped forward with a beautiful Dalmatian, which bounded gracefully into the wagon. Again, the doors were closed, then opened to reveal that the dog had disappeared.

Lastly, Alberto beckoned to Francesca.

"We've got to stop them!" cried Caleb, his voice almost drowned out by the violins. Elodie held out her hand, and Caleb took it, as they raced round the back of the ballroom.

A few people stared in surprise. Elodie met Marnie-Mae's gaze across the candlelit room, and Marnie at once understood what was happening.

"Catch me, I'm fainting!" she bellowed, collapsing dramatically and knocking poor Kit over as she fell. Luckily, years of skating had made them both hardy, and neither of them were even slightly hurt. But at once everyone around them, including Alberto, turned to stare. And in that moment Elodie and Caleb scrambled into the wagon, flattening themselves against the floor.

The violins continued, whipping the crowd

into a frenzy as Francesca obediently led Delphi to the wagon and kissed her nose as the mythical creature stepped inside. The doors closed and there was silence and darkness. Elodie could feel the unicorn's powerful heart beating.

Delphi lowered her head to Caleb, her eyes glittering in the dim light as she ruffled his hair with her nose. Suddenly a trapdoor opened beneath them, and they were tumbling through the ballroom floor on to a large and rather prickly haystack. The trapdoor closed above their heads, sealing them into some sort of underground cellar.

Delphi stood up, looking rather disgruntled. In the murky dark, they spotted the nightingale perched peacefully on a rafter, and the Dalmatian curled up in the corner, watching them curiously.

"We have to set you free," said Elodie gently to Delphi, and the unicorn whinnied her understanding, her horn glinting fiercely.

"This way!" cried Caleb, running off down a little tunnel. Elodie, Delphi, the nightingale and the Dalmatian all followed him through the shadowy dark.

They passed ancient wine cellars and storage rooms full of strange antiques, until finally the air turned damp and they saw the silvery shine of moonlight ahead. Together they broke out of the tunnel on to a beach of soft silvery sand.

It took Elodie a moment to get her bearings, but when she did she shuddered. "It's the beach from my dream," she whispered urgently.

The nightingale swooped towards freedom. The Dalmatian raced for safety. The unicorn raised her horn in anger. For there, striding furiously towards them, was Alberto Stregone and he was holding a lasso of crackling blue lightning.

CHAPTER FOURTEEN
A TERRIBLE TRADITION

Delphi reared up powerfully, but Alberto didn't falter.

"Wait!" cried Elodie in desperation as Caleb threw himself bravely in front of Delphi, whispering to her – begging her – to disappear.

But the unicorn would not leave, her eyes flashing like sea pearls as she searched the beach for Francesca, her heart beating with loyalty and love.

"Yes, you wait right there!" came a familiar voice as Marnie-Mae, Joni and Francesca herself pulled up by the beach on a little pink moped, closely followed by Sophia and Kit in a mint-green moped, and a rather windswept Rufus in the sidecar.

Alberto looked furious at being disturbed, but

then he caught sight of his granddaughter and his face froze in shock.

"What's happening?" asked the little girl and everyone's heart quailed. "I thought Delphi would be waiting outside! You said she'd come straight back after the show," she said crossly to her great-grandfather.

Caleb was feeling hot and angry. He wanted to shout: "Your great-grandpa is a crook who sacrifices unicorns!" But he realized just how much the truth would harm Francesca, so instead he yelled, "He only wants Delphi for her horn to use in the shop – to enchant all the handbags!"

Francesca shook her head in disbelief, but then she took in the lightning lasso and the way her unicorn was rearing up wildly.

"Is this true?" she cried, staring ferociously at Alberto.

"It is an old tradition," protested her great-grandfather. "We don't keep our pets for ever! We live in harmony with them, give them all they need, but every fifty years or so, a sacrifice must be made! It's the only way the House of Handbags can continue."

Francesca flew across the sand like a vengeful fairy and stamped hard on Alberto's foot, making him yelp and drop the lasso.

"Francesca, you don't understand," he said desperately, falling to his knees. "I had a unicorn called Leonardo when I was your age. He was sacrificed for the family trade and, though my young heart broke, I got over it. And you will too."

"Don't you dare hurt my unicorn!" she shouted.

At once, Delphi began to speed across the beach, sand and stardust flying up behind her.

"She thinks Francesca's in trouble," said Elodie, terrified that the graceful unicorn was about to give her life for the little girl and run straight into Alberto's lasso.

Alberto staggered to his feet, clutching the lasso he had plucked from the sand. "I won't hurt her —" he tried to bargain with his granddaughter — "I'll just remove her horn."

"That will kill her!" cried Kit.

Quick as a flash, Sophia whispered to Rufus and he dashed over the sand, much faster than anyone had ever seen him move. With a great growl, he knocked the lasso out of Alberto's hands, far enough away that it was completely out of reach this time.

Delphi was still charging, her horn outstretched and now pointed straight at Alberto.

He was an old man without a weapon and Delphi could easily overpower him, wound him with her horn.

Elodie closed her eyes and reached out to the unicorn with her mind. She felt a flash and a flicker of sparks and fury, and she begged Delphi, *Please stop! Please don't harm Alberto!* But Delphi, in her soul, was wild and wouldn't listen.

Then Elodie felt a warm hand ever so gently take hold of hers. She didn't dare open her eyes to smile at Caleb; she just calmly stood still and let his thoughts join hers so they both sang to the unicorn through the voice of their minds.

Please don't hurt Francesca's great-grandfather – it will break her heart.

Reluctantly, Delphi's hooves slowed and she swerved round Alberto and Francesca, just leaving enough time for the little girl to leap on to her back

before they galloped away back to the streets of Venice.

There was a moment of stillness where the waves sparkled and the stars shone. Alberto gave an exhausted sigh.

Joni stepped forward and offered him a hand, which he begrudgingly took as he stood up and dusted the sand off his trousers.

"Allow us to properly introduce ourselves," said Joni.

Alberto squinted at her bitterly, but Joni ignored his accusing stare and continued. "This is Marnie-Mae, my daughter, and her friend Kit. And over there are Elodie and Caleb, two exceptional Unicorn Seekers. They are the ones who were drawn to Delphi in a dream and knew she needed protecting."

Alberto wrinkled his nose in distrust as the Unicorn Seekers slowly padded over.

"We read all about you in our research," Kit said, smiling.

"And we know you had a very special bond with a unicorn when you were young," added Marnie-Mae.

"So we're asking you to please spare Delphi's life,

otherwise we will take her with us back to South London," said Elodie courageously.

Alberto had a strange look in his eye, as if a childhood memory was stirring somewhere in his soul.

"I just wanted to protect my handbag emporium," he mumbled sadly. "I shan't be around for ever and once I'm gone how will my family succeed without unicorn dust?"

Joni beamed at him. "Your handbags are exquisite. I'm sure you'll find a way."

Alberto gave an unimpressed snort, but didn't argue.

"Please," he muttered, "will you help me find my granddaughter, so I can say sorry?"

"Only if you promise not to hurt Delphi," said Elodie seriously, her hair crackling.

"I swear on my company," said Alberto, wiping a tear from his eye. "It is almost as important to me as my beloved family. My precious Francesca, she is the future and I will do anything to ensure her legacy."

"And you did it all for the love of a unicorn," Sophia said proudly.

They walked together up the beach to a late-night cafe that was serving espresso and gelato. Everyone removed their spectacular masks, apart from Caleb who preferred the sense of mystery his brought him.

"Perhaps you could advertise the Venetia House of Handbags globally – and for free. All we need is a snappy ad campaign and a magical idea," said Joni thoughtfully.

"What is your idea?" Alberto enquired, sipping his coffee.

"Well, if Elle and Caleb – and Francesca – agree, I thought perhaps we could use Delphi in promotional pictures. With your handbags."

Caleb put his hands on his hips crossly.

"Everyone already thinks Delphi being a unicorn is a circus trick," said Marnie. "Like all those people at the ball who were filming it on their phones. So it wouldn't make much difference to put her in an advert – just tell people it's a special effect."

Caleb was quiet a long while.

"I'll speak to Maman," said Elodie. "Make sure everything's done properly and the Ministry of Mythical Protectors agree."

Caleb gave the tiniest incline of his head, which was not quite a nod but not a no either.

"The most important person to ask is Francesca, and of course we'll need Delphi to agree too," he said softly, and everyone nodded in agreement.

"I'd better go and apologize to her. Explain to my family what's really been going on all these years," Alberto said as he stood up to leave. "Just one more question?" he asked, turning back to stare at them sharply over his shoulder. "How on earth did you get into the ball?"

Kit grinned. "With the help of the Speranza family."

Alberto chortled in surprise. "Perhaps it's time I apologized to them as well," he muttered as he went on his way.

Caleb watched him go, and in the distance he was sure he spotted a little horse-shaped shadow flit between the streetlamps and then disappear into the courtyard of a shabby-looking hotel, its sign overgrown with ivy. But Caleb didn't need to read it, for he was certain it would say Views of Venice, Skylar's home… He gave a sharp little sigh as he realized that this was goodbye. The Surf Dancer was where she should be, and now she would remain there with her sister Delphi.

"Farewell," he whispered, then followed his friends into the night.

As the moon shone down in magnificent silver, and after many pistachio ice creams and salty chips were eaten in honour of Delphi, the Unicorn Seekers made their way back. They were still wide-eyed with hope and the thrill of the adventure, so it was rather a delight to find Francesca and Delphi waiting in a pool of moonlight outside their hotel.

Francesca's costume was gone, and Delphi looked very much like a horse, except for the shell-pink hooves and the odd glimmer when moonlight bounced off her dagger-sharp horn.

"Thank you for helping me and saving my unicorn," said the little girl warmly. "How can I ever repay you?"

"Funnily enough," cried Marnie-Mae, "we've got some great ideas for promoting the House of Handbags!"

And so, as clocks all over the city of Venice struck

midnight, a new plan was formed. One where Delphi, Francesca and all the Unicorn Seekers of South London would appear in the very first advert for the Venetia House of Handbags.

The shoot would take place right before they went home and would have a 'carnival' theme with everyone in their costumes from the ball. It would be a thoroughly modern angle to bring in a younger generation.

The House of Handbags had never attempted anything quite like this, but once Alberto appointed Joni as the company's new head of PR – providing her and Marnie-Mae with a guest apartment in central Venice whenever they needed to visit – things moved very quickly.

Elodie spoke at length with Maman, who cleared everything with her network. And Stephano, a talented artist as well as a historian, took the photos while Sophia attended to costumes and styling.

Even Loreta Speranza made an appearance, still dressed in her emerald-green gown and huge velvet hat.

All in all, it was a wildly successful campaign, and soon there were rumours of a collaboration with the Speranza shoe company.

But, most importantly for Elodie, Marnie-Mae, Kit and Caleb, there was now an agreement in place between the two families to protect Surf Dancers or any other unicorns who found their way to the beaches of Venice or indeed elsewhere in Italy.

Even though Elodie's heart still felt tender from saying farewell to Skylar, she knew whenever the wondrous unicorn returned to these waters, she would be safe, all because of her, the Unicorn Seekers and Francesca, and that felt softly magical.

THE PALACE OF CRYSTAL INFORMATION FORUM

Your go-to place for events, community picnics, volunteer gardening, park maintenance, parakeet nesting and general news.

Strange friend from France

My family and I have recently returned from a holiday to Bordeaux. On the way home, we were quite charmed to discover a rogue little pony in our Eurostar carriage. It instantly made friends with our daughter, who claims it was a unicorn! Oh, how sweet, we thought. When the journey came to an end, the little horse strangely vanished. We were sad to say goodbye, but then yesterday my daughter declared she had seen the same horse in this very park. Has anyone else spotted a sandy-coloured horse with grey eyes?

@TwoTiredMums

Spotted by the lake

My son and I have seen a little horse that fits this description, up by the fishing lake. That area's mostly deserted apart from some very keen fisher folk who are out there in all weathers. The odd thing is, we saw the little horse around sunset and maybe it was shadows, or the sun in our binoculars, but for a fleeting moment it looked just like a unicorn.

We left some gluten-free treats from the Feather and Fern for it. They really are the best in all of South London – and we're sure that little horse would agree.

@BirdSpotterBill

Little wild horse

We haven't seen any horses in the park, but my kids and I did have a charming encounter with a similar-sounding little wild horse on the overnight train from Venice to Paris. It climbed on to one of our bunk beds! My children fell completely in love and were even asking if they could keep it. But by morning the horse had vanished quite mysteriously. It made for an unforgettable train ride! They'll be in the park all summer with their granddad and will definitely keep an eye out.

@DreamDesignSuzy

Prints in the sand

Hey, hey!

Has anyone considered it might be an actual unicorn! Ha ha! That would be awesome. Remember those shell-shaped prints that people (including me!) spotted in the sand? Well, I found more around the beach hut. They looked kind of unique and cool – maybe they belong to a new breed of horse? Who knows?

Either way, I think this horse has got great taste. The Feather and Fern do make the best gluten-free snacks ever! Also, my nephew told me there are some kids called the Unicorn Seekers who run a blog about this sort of thing! Maybe drop them a line?

@AlwaysAtTheBeach

CHAPTER FIFTEEN
THE SUNRISE SURPRISE

At six minutes to sunrise in the vast city of London, when the sky can turn from brightest blue to golden grey in the blink of an eye, Elodie Lightfoot peeked out from behind her velveteen curtains at the lovely leafy park opposite her flat.

The summer breeze was warm against the windows and the sky was a perfect cornflower blue. The scent of Parfum de Rose and gluten-free blueberry muffins drifted in from the kitchen where she could hear her parents laughing.

It felt so good to be home – even though she still felt a little heartbroken from saying farewell to Skylar.

"Six minutes till we leave, Elle. You almost ready?" Max called.

Elodie sat up, smoothing her mass of spiralling ringlets into a ponytail. Hardly noticing as the little darts of lightning tingled on her fingers.

Exactly six minutes later, the three of them crept down the stairs, past the Singhs' flat, with armfuls of blueberry muffins, boxes of buttery soft croissants, oatmeal owl biscuits and flasks of coconut milk, all for the Feather and Fern.

"It's perfect weather for croissants," Max said cheerfully as they opened the bright blue door and stepped out into the day.

"You say that every morning, Dad!" Elodie giggled as they made their way to the park.

After Elodie and her parents had set up the van, gobbled their way through some gluten-free muffins – and oat-milk lattes, for the grown-ups – the park was starting to come alive with people enjoying the summer sunshine. Marnie-Mae came soaring over the tarmac on her roller skates, sweeping Elodie into a hug.

"You have to come with me right now," she said.

"It's kind of urgent. Rishi's called a meeting by the beach-volleyball courts."

Elodie pulled on her rainbow-laced roller skates and flew after Marnie towards her friends. She high-fived Kit and Caleb and ruffled Rufus's ears as they all turned and raced across the park – a stream of joy and wheels whizzing all the way to the sports centre.

The courts were empty. There was no one there but Rishi and the beach-volleyball coach's little dog, Luna.

Speeding down to the sand, they slipped off their skates and hugged their much-missed friend.

"What's so urgent? Is there another unicorn that needs our help?" asked Kit, getting his notebook out. It was overflowing with facts and figures and sketches and stories from their Venetian adventure.

Elodie peered across the empty golden sand and spotted Caleb. He was strolling happily

across it with his shoes on, Rufus at his side. And, despite the sunshine, he still proudly wore his winter-themed mask. It really suited him.

Next to Caleb's footprints were the tracks of magpies, foxes and midnight cats.

Then Elodie's heart caught in her throat, her hair dancing with wild blue energy, for there in the dew-kissed sand were a set of prints in the shape of seashells.

Skylar.

"Where is she?" she gasped, a moment before the others spotted the little shell prints.

Rishi beckoned to them and they all squeezed into the beach hut and peered behind the sofa.

And there, quietly dozing like a sleeping princess, was their beautiful friend.

Elodie knelt down and touched the unicorn's sea-foam mane, her heart swelling with joy. Skylar blinked a sleepy grey eye, and gently nuzzled Elodie's palm.

"How did she get here?" asked Kit.

"Guys, I think I know – I just checked the blog." Marnie-Mae was beaming. "She's been having an epic adventure!"

"I thought she lived in Venice with Delphi?" said Kit.

Marnie-Mae shrugged. "I guess she really enjoys travelling!"

"Maybe Skylar lives in Venice some of the time and spends the rest of the year wherever she chooses?" Caleb added.

"She arrived two days ago and has mostly been asleep during the day," Rishi explained. "But she loves going out at night and running through the park or splashing in the fishing lake."

"Has anyone else noticed her? Do you think she can stay here safely?" asked Elodie.

"Sure." Rishi grinned. "No one uses this little hut during the day, and she's got the whole park to herself at night."

"What about the guy who owns Luna?" asked Elodie, dreamily putting her arms round Skylar's neck as she stepped out of the beach hut, shaking her beautiful mane.

"He hasn't noticed her yet. And I don't think he'd mind. I've been coming to beach-volleyball training in exchange for looking after Luna. It's so much fun! I'll show you."

And so the Unicorn Seekers of South London, one dreamy unicorn and two excited dogs had a little game of beach volleyball to kick-start their summer morning.

Caleb preferred to watch. He loved the sand now, but he wasn't quite ready to run around in it. He just wanted to enjoy it at his own pace and eat a breakfast of gluten-free blueberry muffins.

Nobody noticed him carefully sprinkling crumbs behind him. Nor did they hear a tiny whinny from outside the beach-volleyball courts or spy a creature with mossy-green hooves and an amber horn softly glinting in the sunlight.

"A Nightingale's Heart," Caleb murmured, and he quietly went on his way.

How To Save A Unicorn
Lido Island, Venice

Dear Reader,
Ciao from Italy!

I'm Francesca, and I live in the watery city of Venice.

I'm the youngest member of the famous Venetia House of Handbags, and unicorns have been part of my family for generations.

I'm lucky enough to have been a seeker from a very young age. I've grown up with a mythical Surf Dancer named Delphi who used to live in my great-grandpa's warehouse.

She really is the most beautiful creature I've ever known. It's not just her glittering horn or her wild heart that makes her magical, it's her sea-salt soul and her fierce power, and the speed at which she can run. Which is super fast!

Something very sad was going to happen to Delphi, which would have broken my heart for ever and ever, but Delphi's sister, Skylar, did a brilliant thing!

She took the Eurostar all the way to London and found the Unicorn Seekers of South London, and led them all the way back to Venice so that I could meet them!

They came up with a cunning plan to sneak into my family's world-famous masked ball and rescue Delphi. Because of their courage, her life was saved, and my heart was too.

We both owe them so much.

Delphi will keep on enjoying the beaches of Venice, and Skylar will travel round Europe whenever she wishes, seeing our lovely friends in London and calling in on now and then.

Surf Dancers are very well-adapted unicorns - they also have the power of invisibility. If you happen to spot a horse-shaped shadow or see a unicorn on a late-night train, you too may be a Unicorn Seeker.

Here is what you can do:

- Surf Dancers are very friendly but sometimes shy. The best way to make friends with them is with food. They especially love salty chips, and gelato.

- Let the unicorn come to you. They may try to reach you in your dreams or even turn up in your local park or back garden, so always be ready and keep an open heart.
- Surf Dancers are used to living around people and will want to form a lasting bond, even becoming part of your family, so be sure to keep their secret and don't be surprised if you make a friend for life.
- Lastly, remember that Surf Dancers are magical creatures who might be in danger. If you're worried about one of them, get in touch with the Unicorn Seekers of South London, or visit our shop in Venice and we'll help you protect your unicorn.
  Keep guarding the magic!

Ciao for now,
Francesca xx

ABOUT THE AUTHOR

Cerrie Burnell is an author, actor and ambassador best known for work on CBeebies – a role that has earned her critical recognition and a devoted fan base. During her time on CBeebies she has broken down barriers, challenged stereotypes and overcome discrimination to become one of the most visible disabled presenters on kids' TV.

Cerrie is the author of fourteen children's books including *Snowflakes*, which she adapted for the stage with Oxford Playhouse in 2016 and the Harper series, which was a World Book Day title in 2016, as well as creating her one-woman show the *Magical Playroom,* which premiered at the Edinburgh fringe in 2013.

Since leaving CBeebies, Cerrie has appeared in the BBC continuing drama *Doctors* and made the eye-opening documentary *Silenced* for the BBC. Her non-fiction book *I Am Not A Label* was an Amazon

US twenty best children's non-fiction book of 2020 and was the overall children's choice winner of the SLA Information Book Awards 2021.

Wilder Than Midnight was Indie Book of the Month, and Blackwell's Book of the Month for May 2022, and was shortlisted for the first-ever Adrien Prize and the well-established Sheffield Book Awards.

Cerrie recently worked for the BBC behind the scenes as their ambassador for disability with the creative diversity unit. She is currently dreaming up new ideas and drinking mint hot chocolate.

Photo by Lynda Kelly